Iveliz Explains It All

ANDREA BEATRIZ ARANGO

Random House New York

Text copyright © 2022 by Andrea Beatriz Arango
Jacket art copyright © 2022 by Abigail L. Dela Cruz
Interior illustrations copyright © 2022 by Alyssa Bermudez

Visit us on the Web! rhcbooks.com

Educators and librarians, for a variety of teaching tools, visit us at RHTeachersLibrarians.com

Library of Congress Cataloging-in-Publication Data is available upon request.
ISBN 978-0-593-56397-7 (trade) — ISBN 978-0-593-56398-4 (lib. bdg.) —
ISBN 978-0-593-56399-1 (ebook)

Printed in the United States of America
10 9 8 7 6 5 4 3 2 1
First Edition

Para mi papi . . . thank you for still visiting my dreams.

Second Chances

Why is it that principals
love giving second chances?
Love reminding me they were kids too?
Love acting like they're doing me a favor,
doing my mom a favor,
by sitting me down all serious
and asking what they can do?

Well, guess what.
This is seventh grade now,
and I don't need anyone's help but my own.
I've moved on from **everything**
that happened,
I've made lists and I've made goals,
and if I'm in the principal's office,
you can 100% bet
that it wasn't my fault.

Who Can You Trust?

If you ask my teachers,
they might say I'm a liar,
because I always insist
things are not my fault.

And if you ask my mom,
she might say que soy una dramática,
'cause she used to sometimes think
my old panic attacks
were about getting attention
and not an anxious brain response.

But, Journal,
don't listen to them,
because these right here?
They're my true inner thoughts.
And if you can't trust a girl and her poems,
well,
who CAN you trust?

Back It Up

Mami gave you to me last week—
hardcover, gold trim.
Like my TikTok wouldn't be good enough
if I really wanted to speak.

She says it's to encourage my "creativity." . . .
Dizque pa ver if I can actually get some writing in.

But I know what it is, really.
Mimi (my abuelita) is coming real soon, and
Mami's worried it'll make me switch back.
Like my grandma will somehow
fly me through time,
before the pills and Dr. Turnip,
back when things were all out of whack.

P-o-r   f-a-v-o-r.
I'm twelve.
And Mimi has had Alzheimer's forever—
I mean years and years.

I'm not gonna get a panic attack
just 'cause she forgets my name.

Si fuese por eso,

I'd get them every day at school.

'Cause Listen

The end of elementary school?

Worst time of my life.

And the start of middle school?

I just wasn't quite right.

But this year?

YO VOY A MI.

Because ¿yo?

Yo soy una dura. Yo soy latina.

Me?

I am   I-V-E-L-I-Z

                  Margarita Snow Medina.

And that's EE-VEH-LEASE, not Ivy-Liz,

EE-VEH to family and friends.

Aunque even though I've explained

the "veh" is short

like in *pet,*

it seems nobody ever remembers

to twist their mouths the right way.

Like in that spoken word poem by Elizabeth Acevedo

and Pages Matam

and G Yamazawa

(the real spoken poetry OGs),

except, unlike them,

most times I talk when I shouldn't

and am quiet when I should screech,

so maybe I need some lessons on figuring out

when to hold my thoughts in.

ISBI

It means:

> In School Behavior Intervention.

It means:

> I messed up my second chance.

But what was I supposed to do?

I was telling Amir about Mimi moving in
(Amir is my only friend),
and then Jessica and Justin G.
heard me
and Jessica was all: Omg whaaaaaat?
That's so sad.
Is she coming here illegally
or are you, like, getting her a visa?
'Cause, you know,
we're all about immigration, but,
do it right.

And I swear my hair crackled,
frizzy curls spitting fire,
'cause this is exactly what I was talking about before.
Jessica and Justin G.? They NEVER get in trouble,
even though they're the ones being terrible
practically nonstop.

I told them they were racists,

and maybe a few other words too,

and then I was shoving Jessica to the ground

before anyone had a chance

to alert the adults in the school.

So all I can do now, Journal,

is hope the front office

doesn't call Mami right away.

'Cause Amir seeing me get in trouble?

That's plenty enough for one day.

I don't need to cause any more disappointment.

No gracias. Not today.

Not My Job

It just gets so tiring.

I mean it's not even that hard to learn.

Puerto Rico is a US territory (sort of like DC?).

Which means Mami is a US citizen,

even though she grew up going to school in Spanish

and eating arroz con pernil.

She always says how lucky she is.

How all she had to do was grab her passport and board a plane,

how she has so much PRIVILEGE

because she didn't have to risk her life

risk her money

risk her home and family and job,

all to come work her butt off

in the continental United States.

At school I did a whole presentation

(post Hurricane María)

'cause my school was doing a canned food drive.

But do Jessica and Justin G. remember what I talked about?

Remember my pictures and facts and slides?

Of course not.

Because all "Hispanics" are "illegal" to them,

and "illegal" always means "bad."

Dad Thinks He's Funny

He sees me,

scribbling angry poems as I sit on the living room couch.

Says he was a poet too.

Supuestamente y que in college,

and that's how he swept Mami off her feet.

Later, I ask her where the poems at,

but she laughs and says: your daddy?

He never wrote a poem in his life.

Dios mío, she laughs,

¿te imaginas?

Except when I report back to Dad,

Dad winks at me.

Wide.

Wider.

Girrrrrl, he drawls out, accent thick and warm,

full of crawfish and Louisiana swamp:

There's more to poetry than words.

And I groan and fake puke,

because there's nothing worse than

thinking about your dad being all romantic—

except maybe thinking about your mom,

all young and lipstick on,

falling for all his flirts.

Still. I Can't Complain.

Kids at my school?

They're always whining

que si

Dad this

que si

Dad that,

but my dad?

He's the best.

And there's no one I'd rather

go to Costco with,

fight over a bag of popcorn with,

double over laughing at his pranks with

than my funny

life of the party

prankster of a

dad.

Mami, Though?

That's another story.

Like how today she wants me

to get Mimi's room ready,

which I *will*,

I promise I will,

but how is she gonna get annoyed at me

when SHE'S the one who told me about

       ~Rebelde~

(which she used to watch when she was a kid).

Yeah, it's cheesy,

but that's what makes it so fun.

Mami is always telling me to smile more anyways,

so you'd think she'd want me watching more TV

and cracking up a storm

(especially when it seems like she still hasn't received

The Call).

But no,

it's always Ive, I said NOW

      always Ive, ¿me escuchaste?

           always Ive, if you don't get up

              ~ahora mismo~

because apparently obedience isn't obedience

if there's even the slightest delay.

María

I'm finally cleaning Mimi's future room,

because at the end of the day,

she's one of my favorite people,

even if I haven't seen her since María,

aka categoría cinco.

Hurricane María,

my dear Journal,

fue una BEEEEP.

As in,

it's the one time Mami didn't pull my ears

for cussing in front of her.

'Cause that's how bad

it turned out to be.

My aunts didn't have power for five months.

(And they were the ones better off!)

Which should tell you something

about everything

'cause that's a long time to not have a phone.

Dad mailed a generator for Mimi

so she could have AC,

'cause the island was all out of generators

and Mimi is old

13

(well, old enough),

plus she was already sick.

But then Mami convinced him we needed to go too,

y que pa vivirlo en familia.

So I packed granola bars into

every available pocket of my backpack

('cause your girl is *not* about

that Vienna sausage/Spam life),

pero Mami said I needed to work on being grateful

and she dumped them all out.

Hello? Who my granola bars hurting?

It Honestly Wasn't That Scary

Mimi's Alzheimer's, I mean.

Puerto Rico was freaking unbelievable.

Blue tarps stretching farther than the eye can see—

literally whole mountains speckled with blue roofs

and roads broken in half like they were twigs.

I mean, my aunts stood in line for hours

en el Texaco

just to fill up a plastic gas can with fuel.

Either that or water—

small cases and jugs that wouldn't last them a week.

But Mimi was okay.

Worse than the last time we were there,

pero no taaaan mal.

She knew I was her Ive,

even if she forgot we didn't live on the island.

That I was only there for summers,

and only 'cause we saved all year long.

But that was okay too,

you know?

I liked leading a double life with her,

getting to be Iveliz Margarita:

nacida y criada en Borikén.

A true boricua,

and not the half gringa con pelo malo

I know people call me in my neighborhood back home.

So, really,

Mami can panic all she wants,

and give me all the journals she wants,

but I'm not scared to see Mimi.

It hasn't been *that* long since our visit.

How could she possibly have changed that much?

ISBI (cont.)

If you've never been in IS-BEE,
it's kind of hard to explain.

You basically sit at a table

and wait

     and wait

          and wait

               and wait
until a "good" kid from your teacher's class
brings something for you to do.

So sure, *sometimes* there's a worksheet
but most of the time there's nothing,
because teachers are too busy teaching
(which I get)
to make new work for those in ISBI.

I mean literally the whole point of this is to punish
without suspending kids outside,
but then they send me to a room
where I miss school anyways
and expect me not to fall behind.

Seventh-Grade Goals: An Official List

- ☐ Do what Mami says (the first time she asks)
- ☐ Help Mimi settle in
- ☐ Be more social?
- ☐ **DON'T GET SENT TO ISBI AGAIN**

She Got the Call

Aka Mami grounded me.
'Cept she's not very creative
'cause she always does the same thing:
holds out her long piano-fingered right hand
and curls it in and out like she's squeezing a huge lemon.

Translation? Dame tu teléfono.
Like that's my only form of communication.
(LOL)
Not that I'm about to correct her.

Yo no soy boba, and I know what'll happen
if she finds out I can Google Chat on my school Chromebook,
that I can still video call Amir late at night.

She'll hold out both hands and squeeze some more invisible
    lemons,
and then it'll be my phone in one hand
and my Chromebook in the other.

Speak Up, Not Out

                                        That's what Dad says
                              when he comes over to lecture me.
                                        Speak up, not out.
                              Like I can control my anger so easy,
                    like it's just a volume switch I can wiggle up and down.

                                    He says that's what his mamma told him,
                                        and so that's what he's telling me.
                                    That my mixed butt needs to be careful
                                    (even if my face is closer to Mami's white).

We've had this conversation before,
so I try not to roll my eyes,
but they must've still rolled a little, because Daddy smiles.

                                        Eres igual que tu mami, he says.
                                              Strong. Passionate.

But he must be talking about a different mami,
'cause I've never seen MY mami get passionate about anything.
Always rules this and rules that and a serious face.

When she says "sigue"
real calm and low,
I DON'T sigue.
You get me?

Video Chats

I pull Amir up on my laptop

while I fold laundry in my room.

He's organizing his book collection,

so we take turns picking songs on YouTube

to hum along to,

to help time move faster

                              . . . slower . . .

as we clean up the rooms.

And it's nice. You know?

Even Amir's little brother is running around.

Mami thinks it's stupid,

how Amir and I are always on screen

but not always talking,

pero hello,

sometimes kids want company too,

and it's not my fault she always leaves me alone

(or grounded)

with either too much

or nothing to do.

First Name Unknown

Wanna know something real messed up?

When my friend Amir came here from Afghanistan

there was some sort of error with his name.

So his school documents and all his records say Amir Fnu,

which means Amir First Name Unknown,

even though Amir is his first name and his last name IS known.

So whenever we start a new school year

the teachers are all: Mr. Fnu?

(pronounced FFF-nu),

even though his last name is Nishat

and every kid at school knows that.

And Amir just laughs it off.

Laughs it off!

Because he is Amir,

and he says what's the point.

But honestly it bothers me just as much

as when they mess up my own name.

Like, hello?

How hard is it to ask kids what they want to be called,

and then learn it?

Dad Thinks He's Funny, Part II

I showed Dad some of my poems, Journal,
and he laughed and said he could write poems like that too.
Laughed and asked if that's how Gen Z wrote poetry,
all random thoughts and no rhyme.

But I don't see what's so funny.
You're MY journal and they're MY poems.
And if it's not for school,
who cares if I write in "quatrains" or have "rhyme schemes"?
Not me, that's who.

Plus, I've read books in verse.
He can't trick me—
I know there aren't rules when it's a diary,
just like there aren't any rules
when Safia Elhillo or Sarah Kay
or Mahogany L. Browne steps onstage.

OMG he just came in my room and saw me writing and was all:

I am your daddy. Line break.
You are my lve. Line break.
And every eye roll means you love me more.
Line break.
Than you ever thought you could.
End poem.

I threw a pillow straight at him but I missed.

Of course.

Mimi Is Here!

And the room cleaning passed inspection
(gracias a Dios),
and though Mimi seems kinda off,
it's not really that surprising,
porque obvio, this is a huge change!

I mean,
in PR she had a square house with a big yard,

       o

   m n

  n   t

u   e

with hills growing avocados big as Dad's hands.

There were mangos, and guanábanas, and plátanos,
and those ugly brown oranges
I've only ever seen grow
on the road leading up to her house.

But here? We're on the third floor.
Half the windows are jammed so hard they don't open,
and the rooms are all stuffy and carpeted beige.
O sea, PR to Baltimore?
Mimi <u>definitely</u> got a downgrade.

Fun Things I Want to Do with Mimi

- Cook   *because I love to, but Mami never has the time to show me how*

- Garden   *because it reminds me of PR but Mami can't show me how*

- Talk!   *because Mimi has all the family stories and the tea*

- Cuddle   *because Mami is not very touchy, and I miss Dad's hugs something fierce*

Tania

I'm talking with Mimi after dinner
and she's all:
Mi vida, qué grande estás.
Séptimo grado—ni me lo imagino.
Que raro pensar que ya mi Tania
es casi teenager y no mi bebita no más.

And I smile and nod, Journal,
and pretend my heart doesn't skip a beat
when Mimi calls me by Mami's name,
porque, hello, Mami did warn me,
and, like,
I've seen pictures of Mami at my age.
We do look alike.
Really, it's an honest mistake.

So when Dad makes eye contact with me,
I shrug and roll my eyes.
'Cause your girl Ive isn't bothered by <u>anything</u>,
you get me?

But still. Tania is a weird way to start.

Mimi's Room

I help Mimi unpack all her clothes—
mostly batas that look like pajamas,
but that I pretend are real clothes
and hang up.
Then I grab her bags and bags of lipsticks
and set them on top of the dresser and the little mirror,
that Mimi immediately insists is too small.

My favorites are her framed pictures, though,
her and Grandpa all serious and posed,
and a different one,
in color,
with all the kids and grandkids
from a few years ago.

The third one shakes me up a bit,
'cause Dad has his arm around Mami all tight,
and walks down memory lane just aren't as fun
when the lane is all jagged and painful and dark.

Metí la pata

I told Amir about the Tania mix-up.

Very casual.

Just threw it in when we were talking at school.

I do that sometimes

when I'm not sure how to feel.

See, Amir is the most chill person I know.

But me? I'm always up and down

like a buttered bag of popcorn.

Sometimes unpopped.

Sometimes burnt to a crisp.

Almost never just right.

The medicine I take every day helps,

sort of (?),

or maybe it's just that I've gotten over all of **that,**

so anyways it's still useful,

de vez en cuando,

to just say something and see how Amir reacts.

To watch his eyes and eyebrows and cheeks

and match them,

like I'm an octopus in camouflage

or I'm wearing a mask.

Except this time,

when I told him,

when I said the thing about Tania and all that,

he nodded very slowly,

put his fork down,

readjusted his glasses,

and said:

Have I ever told you about my grandfather Irfan?

Samosas

My grandfather was supposed to come with us, Amir says. When
we left Afghanistan to go to Turkey to escape all the fights.
But it's not an easy journey, and it's long, and when we got to
Turkey we were asked many questions in many ways to see if we
could pass. Grandpa Irfan, he had dementia, Amir continues, and
it was getting pretty bad, and when the soldiers asked him what
he was doing, he said he was looking for samosas to fry up that
night. The soldiers got mad, Amir says. They thought he was
making fun or . . . I don't know. I was little. Things are blurry
and kinda black. But I know the soldiers hit him, and wouldn't
let him enter, and in the end, my uncle Yunus took Irfan, and
the car, and they left us in Turkey and drove back.

Irfan Is Not Who I Wanted to Hear About, Journal

But of course Amir tells me anyways,

and I write what I can remember later

because it seems important,

it feels important,

that I get it down just right.

Irfan is dead now,

in Afghanistan,

has been for years,

and I don't think Amir told me to scare me

or trigger me,

but to say:

My friend,

I have lived this too

and I am here for you.

It is scary but I have your back.

Except now I still don't know how to feel,

because Mimi is not Irfan,

and I am not Amir.

And maybe Mami was at least like *a quarter* right,

because I'm writing about Mimi in you like she wanted me to

and por favor, Ive, get it together.

You have gardening next,

You

    Will

Be

    Fine.

Hands at Work

Gardening class
is one of my exploratories at school.
An "exploratory" being what they call "specials"
in middle school,
like it'll make us appreciate band more
if it's "an exploration"
and not a class mandated by law.

Anyways, I really like it.
Like . . . like it, like it,
much more than every other class,
even though it means I get dirt under my nails
and Mami is always telling me to paint them,
dizque pa disimular.

But I don't care if people see the dirt.
It means I planted FOOD.
And it reminds me of gardening with Mimi en el monte
and our summers full of
pastelillitos and endless sunshine. . . .
I mean it was a whole mood.

Wait a minute.
OMG I AM A GENIUS.*

*I'm gonna ask Mami if I can start a garden with Mimi on the balcony. Will update soon.

Gandules

Mami said yes,

and Mimi said yes,

but when I asked Mimi what she wanted to grow,

she said gandules.

¡Gandules!

As if we could just walk into Walmart

and buy a pack.

But even though I am positive we can't grow that in Maryland,

Mami told Mimi she would buy some seeds online,

and nobody asked me,

but if they had I would've said:

Mami Mami Mami—don't do Mimi like that.

They're not gonna grow, and then she'll be sad.

But who asked me?

Nobody, that's who.

Never mind that I'M the one in gardening class.

Never mind that it's literally my *only* class that's

going all right.

Ridículo, I tell you.

Just 'cause she's an adult

doesn't mean she's right.

Dinner Is Weird Tonight

We have arroz guisado,

which is my favorite,

with tofu the way I like it—

roasted slow in the oven and hot sauce drenched.

But Mimi is distracted and keeps staring off,

occasionally asking me why I'm not eating meat,

even though me and my sweaty palms

have told her multiple times

that I am vegetarian, and no,

I'm not changing my mind.

I try to hype her up about the garden instead,

pero she's all:

¿Qué jardín, Ive?

and for a minute I stare at her,

because I forget that her brain crinkles

and I'm supposed to remind her and all that.

So I pitch my idea

                    again

and she likes it

                    again

but everything is kinda buzzy and strange,

like I'm stuck in a déjà vu loop

that doesn't know when to end.

Mami says I'm gonna have to be very patient with Mimi

'cause she might forget what I tell her.

A LOT.

And I just shrug and tell Mami

I have plenty of practice with repetition,

because kids at school are idiots,

and I'm basically always giving them

the same lines:

It's EEE-VEH-LEASE.

   EEE-VEH.

      EEE. VEH. LEASE.

Yes, I speak Spanish.

   I speak Spanish.

      YES, I speak.

No, you can't touch my hair

   You can't touch it.

      NO.

And stop telling me to smile.

   Stop telling me.

      Just STOP.

Current Seventh-Grade Goals

- ☐ Do what Mami says (the first time she asks)
- ☑ Help Mimi settle in
- ☐ Be more social?
- ☐ DON'T GET SENT TO ISBI AGAIN
- ☐ Figure out how to grow gandules
- ☐ Be patient with Mimi when I have to repeat myself

Nuh-uh, ni se te ocurra

That's what Mami's voice hisses at me in my head today
when Justin G.
trips me in the hall as I am on my way to math.

I turn around so fast
I literally slap myself in the face with my own hair,
and by the time Jessica turns around too,
all laughing teeth and blond hair and poison eyes,
a crowd of phones has appeared out of nowhere,
recording what I'm sure they think
is bound to be an epic fight.

Ni se te ocurra,
the Mami voice tells me.
But I'm not convinced.
'Cause with the crowd hyping me up,
phones pointing toward us,
there's suddenly nothing I want more
than to connect Justin's face with my fist.

It's weird how fast it can happen.
How I can go from neutral
to revved up
in three seconds flat.

Dr. Turnip

used to tell me it was a

p-h-y-s-i-o-l-o-g-i-c-a-l

reaction, something my body did

to protect me and stay alive.

And maybe that was true *before,*

back when I wasn't 100% right:

back when my heart pounded fast

my skin got hot

and my teeth used to

angrily clench tight.

Today, though, when I see the resource officer,

I remember my list of goals,

and I somehow pull myself out of the

full-out rage I know is coming

and the suspension that would have followed

if I'd melted down and fully let go.

I calm down, obvio,

but I still end up here, in the counselor's office,

where Mrs. Mohr slowly takes off her glasses

and asks me real serious

why my behavior is reverting,

when she thought the anger

was past us and

the fighting

long gone.

Talk to me, EEE-VAY,

she says all sweet,

and the fact that she still can't say my name right

is almost enough to set me off again.

But nobody wants some Dr. Turnip today, Journal.

Ni se te ocurra.

Dr. Turnip: An Explanation

Some moms threaten their kids with a chancla.

Others take away devices or social media

or assign triple chores or something like that.

But my mami? When she's real upset?

She'll bring up Turnip (aka Dr. Alex,

though Turnip better suits his head),

and threaten to call him,

threaten to take me,

which is basically the worst punishment

she could ever give.

And Turnip is fine, I guess.

It's not personal, my hate.

But would you want to do

something no other middle schoolers do?

Would you want to talk to an adult

about everything **wrong** with you

and everything you need to **fix**

so that things are NORMAL

and PERFECT

and OKAY?

Yeah, I thought so.

Everyone Is Against Me, I Swear

Why else would Justin trip me?

Why else would Jessica laugh with glee?

Why else would the school popo take me to the counselor,

who in turn CALLS MAMI,

who then brings up Turnip

for something that wasn't even me?

With the kids it's 'cause I'm mixed

y hablo español.

With the teachers it's my meds,

which they love to blame

when something goes wrong.

With Amir it's sometimes feeling

like I still need to hide.

And at home it's 'cause I'm Daddy's daughter

with no Daddy in sight.

But everywhere?

Everywhere?

You guessed it.

I am alone.

¿Estás bien?

That's what Mami asks at dinner.

But what she means is:

Why are you getting in trouble again?

What she means is:

Do we need to go back to Hopkins Child & Psych?

What she really means is:

Is this about Mimi or Dad?

Mimi Is Working on a Puzzle

And I'm avoiding Mami till bedtime,
'cause she already has my phone,
what she gonna take next?

So I sit next to Mimi to write,
occasionally looking over her progress
and smiling at her
so she'll smile back.

The puzzle is a rain forest one
and I squint at the dull colors and big pieces,
wondering if Mami picked the ugliest one
on purpose, just to make Mimi sad.

El Yunque es más lindo, I tell Mimi,
and she nods.
And I think of all the animals
in the PR rain forest
(of the parrots and lizards and frogs),
but mostly I think of the tourists,
with their fancy hiking sandals and big hats,
and that peeling red skin
always giving them away
no matter how quickly
they try to climb to the top.

Busca a tu papá para que me ayude,
she says after a bit,
and I freeze,
trying hard to figure out
if this is the Alzheimer's or a dream.

But Mimi clucks at me with her mouth
and gestures for me to go,
so I walk to the kitchen
and stand
and sit
and stand again,

wondering where exactly I'm supposed to look for him,
where exactly I'm supposed to go.

Statuesque

¿Estás bien?

Mami asks again when she comes in for a drink.

And I don't say anything,

but she must feel something

because she puts the glass down

without taking a sip.

Iveliz, she says.

Except I am

marble, I am

s t o n e .

(Iveliz)

Like the

legends of

the dog statue

in Puerto Rico

hardening

out of grief

and out of

love.

IVELIZ, she says,

> gripping my
>
> shoulders,
>
> giving me a
>
> s h a k e ,
>
> and so I turn
>
> because my
>
> face isn't
>
> frozen (yet)
>
> and I test out
>
> my voice with a
>
> w h i s p e r
>
> because that's all
>
> I can manage to say.

> Mimi sent me to get
>
> Dad,
>
> I whisper. She told me
>
> to get him. And I—

> But I don't have to
>
> say anything else,
>
> because Mami grabs me
>
> and hugs me

and then my statue skin is broken
and I crumple like a wet piece of paper
into Mami's cold, firm hands.

I Can Hear Them

The walls in our apartment
aren't very thick.

Mami is pretty quiet,
whispery even,
and Mimi too,
but the words still float over into my room.

Remember, Mami?

Iveliz
                                    Therapy
            Try
                          Please try
Triggers
                  Try

49

Amir Nishat, an Acrostic

Artistic

My friend

Intellectual

Relaxed

Needed

Incognito

SOS

Help

Amir

Talk to me

Talk to me

Talk

Dos y dos son cuatro

In bed, I can't stop humming the nursery rhyme
Mimi taught me when I was little,
the one that starts with a girl and her doll
and then moves on to counting and adding,
skipping smaller numbers
in favor of bigger,
odd ones in favor of even.

We used to be a family of three,
and then because of me it became two.
Now Mimi is here and I can't help but think
this is my second chance at home,
the opportunity to fill all the silence
and hurt
and past,
the chance to be forgiven—
not by praying,
but in real life.

And unlike school?
I can't mess this one up.

My Ex-Friend Amir, Unforgiven

Dad thinks I'm being unreasonable.

Says no one can be there for someone 24-7.

But I ignore him because

where was HE last night?

Exactly.

And anyways I don't need anyone.

I got me, myself, and I.

Soy la dura.

But Dad laughs and says I'm no dura,

I'm his little Ive,

and I roll my eyes but don't argue,

because the truth is this dura

wasn't quite hard enough

last night.

And even though Amir is my best friend

and even though he is the kindest person around,

sometimes I wish he knew how to read my mind,

so that he would give me what I want

without me having to ask.

Que llueva, que llueva, la bruja está en la cueva

On Saturday it is pouring when I get up.
Perfect weather for Maizena and Mimi and laughs.
But when I look for Mimi to offer her some,
I find her crying in bed real bad.

Mimi, ¿qué pasa?
I ask her,
because she's been here a week
and in all those days I've never seen her so sad
and so small.

"Es Georges," she whispers,
and even though I don't know who Georges is,
my skin prickles
as I run out the room
and down the hall.

Mami follows me back quick,
and calms Mimi down,
explaining quietly to me
that sometimes storms
remind Mimi of Hurricane María
except the Alzheimer's tricks her
and makes her forget
where (and when) she is.

She helps Mimi to the bathroom
so she can take a nice hot shower,
and tells me that Georges,
he was another hurricane,
one that hit when she was a teen
and they all lived in Caguas.

No fue un María, claro, Mami says.
Pero le arrancó el techo a mi escuela.
And I sigh and go make toast,
and try to imagine a world where
roofs get ripped off schools,
and grandmas wake up twenty years later
still crying about it.

Pastillas

I'm kind of avoiding Amir,
though I don't think he knows it
because he's at his cousin's wedding in DC.

Mimi is doing better,
much better,
and I'm sitting near her doing homework
when she turns and gives me a hard stare.

I smile at her but she doesn't smile back,
her hands slowly pushing her frames
up the bridge of her nose.
Las drogas son malas, she says.

I raise my eyebrows at her.
Yo se, I say,
wondering why Mimi is talking to me about drugs
when I'm basically the most innocent kid
in all of seventh grade.

Yo te vi anoche, she continues,
and I rack my brain to figure out what the heck
she is talking about,
what she saw,
what drugs she thinks I have.

Te vi. After dinner, she says,

as if switching to English will help me get it faster,

will help me connect the dots.

Except it actually does,

because suddenly everything clicks.

Mimi, those aren't drugs. They're my medicine.

I take pills every night.

Mimi looks suspiciously at me,

and I roll my eyes.

Son medicina, I say again. Para mi depresión

y mi PTSD.

Bah. Tu no tienes esas cosas, she says,

waving her hand and looking at her puzzle.

But I do, Mimi, I say, confused.

The doctor gave them to me to help my brain.

I have PTSD. Like you after the hurricane? And the—

Exacto, Mimi says, sitting back all satisfied.

I don't take pills when it rains.

Las pastillas son para los locos y tu no eres loca.

Just throw them away.

And I smile and nod

because what else can I do,

but suddenly Mimi's voice

feels as sharp as Jessica's or Justin G.'s,

suddenly her presence

isn't as comforting as I'd first thought,

and for the first time I worry

this addition to our family

isn't going to fill any gaps.

Because if pills are only for crazy people,

and even Mimi

after a whole category five hurricane

doesn't need them,

then really,

what am I?

Monday Morning Is Quiet

I guess I underestimated how much I usually talk to Amir.

But at lunch, this girl I've seen before
walks by the tree I'm leaning against
and stops,
long shiny black hair and puffy eyes,
her face both a question
and a sort of friendship mirage.

I can tell she's upset,
and it's not that she's choosing me
so much as the fact that
the bathrooms are probably all full
and it's either the cafeteria tables
or me and the trees outside.

I don't really want company either,
but I'm not made of stone,
so I pat the ground next to me
and she sits,
and I try to remember the last time
I talked to someone
who wasn't Amir or Mimi or Mami or Dad.

We don't talk, really,

so I guess it doesn't count.

She sniffles and watches the squirrels.

I eat my rice and keep my head down.

But when the bell rings, I clear my throat and help her up.

And she smiles and says: Akiko.

And my heart grows two sizes bigger

when I answer: Iveliz.

Gandules, II

They arrive on Tuesday morning,
which means Mami paid extra for fast shipping,
even though I know that'll mean more shifts at Safeway
and less ice cream late at night.

So after school we all crowd into the car
and go to Home Depot,
where Mimi picks out deep circular pots,
her smile wide and loud,
probably imagining rows and rows of pigeon peas
all lining up in the house.

Mimi and Mami talk and talk,
the kind of rapid-fire Spanish
that makes the containers in their hands
swing around
as I struggle to keep up.

And who's stuck carrying the huge bag of potting soil?
¡Cómo si yo fuera the strongest!
The struggle is real,
and before I know it
my hoodie is covered in dirt
from the bottom to the top.

I throw the dusty bag on the floor

in frustration,

try to shake off all the black crumbs,

and then regret it two seconds later

when Mami's voice snaps:

¿Pero cuántos años tú tienes? Iveliz, hazme el favor.

Like she doesn't know this is my favorite hoodie.

Like she doesn't know it's the one Dad got me to match his.

It's **HER** dirt that's on **ME**

but somehow I'm the one who's wrong?

I bite my lip, hard,

and you would think Mami was part bruja

the way she can read my angry swirling thoughts,

'cause she clucks her tongue at me,

and reminds me

that without the dirt there's no garden

and I'm the one who cooked this project up.

So I think of Turnip's old strategy and count:

10

9

8

7

6

5

4

3

2

1

and then pick up the dirt again.

And when Mimi puts her soft arm around me,

I forgive her for everything and relax into her warmth.

Mimi's Hands Are Smart, Journal

She shows me how to dip my fingers in,
how to make little nests in the packed dirt:
cozy homes for the big seeds.

She puts her hands on mine
and they feel rough but soft,
like a peach mixed with a kiwi
(a piwi?)
and it feels so nice on the sunny balcony
that I stop and just look at her.
And for a minute I wish that there was no Mami
and no Alzheimer's
and no PTSD
and it was just Mimi and me.
Mimi and I,
because the only person who used to make me feel
this way was Dad, and
even though I know Mami tries,
she's just not as snuggly as I want.

So when Mimi stops and looks at me,
when she kisses my cheek and pulls me close,
there must be some brave truth spell in the air,
because I lean into her smell
and whisper:

¿Tú crees en fantasmas?
and let my secret out.

Mimi thinks about it.
Really thinks about it,
which makes me feel good
and important
and smart.
And then she says that she doesn't know about ghosts,
but she does believe in guardian angels,
which are basically the only kinds of ghosts
Catholicism allows.

I scrunch up my nose
and Mimi laughs and pets my head.
But really, isn't Mimi onto something?

Porque la verdad es que,
if we really break it down,
look at the why and the what and the when,
aren't guardian angels just ghosts
for people who need the story
to be about them?

Amir, Forgiven

Partly because I want to ask him about Akiko.
But mostly 'cause I know Dad is right.

I'm sorry I wasn't there, Amir says on Google Meet,
and I'm sorry your dad wasn't either.

And I nod, because I love my dad
but I also hate him too,
and Amir is the only one who gets it
and seems to always know
what to say and do.

It's okay, I say.
Dad apologized también.
And then I change the subject and ask about Akiko,
but Amir looks at me for so long
that I think the video on my Chromebook is frozen,
and I give it a little shove and a shake.

I'm here, he says.
And he is,
but so is his worried face,
all green eyes squinting
and forehead crinkling
and questions I know he wants to ask
but he doesn't say.

Akiko, you know her?

I ask.

And he finally smiles, just halfway,

And I let out the breath I didn't know I was holding

because everything is fine,

we will be fine,

everything will stay the same.

Things I Now Know About Akiko: A List

1. She does Brazilian jiujitsu.
2. She is older than me. Thirteen. Eighth grade.
3. She has a mom. She has a dad.
4. She knows three languages.
5. She transferred here from Westminster.
6. She likes fashion and design.
7. Her mom is Japanese and her dad is German.
8. She was crying because a group of boys said her lunch smelled gross and threw it out.

Current Seventh-Grade Goals

- ☐ Do what Mami says (the first time she asks)
- ☑ Help Mimi settle in
- ☐ Be more social? Idk
- ☑ DON'T GET SENT TO ISBI AGAIN
- ☐ Figure out how to grow gandules
- ☑ Be patient with Mimi when I have to repeat myself

I Promise Amir I Won't Hit Anyone

But it's kind of a stupid promise,

because revenge is about so much more than violence,

and if I'm sneaky enough, I won't get caught.

I know the risks—it's not like I don't—

but wouldn't this be the perfect way

to get Akiko to be my friend?

For me to finally get to be the one helping

and not the one being helped?

To have a totally normal friendship

with someone who doesn't know

fifth- and sixth-grade Ive,

only the amazing seventh-grade Ive

who got back at those boys?

So, really, if we're being super technical,

this is kind of Amir's fault,

because what he should have made me promise

is that I would drop it

and just let the whole thing go.

Payback

Since the boys threw away Akiko's food,
I decide my prank has to be food related,
obviously, and stinky too.
So I spend all of Wednesday
trying to figure out the perfect revenge food.

Then Mami
(Dios la bendiga)
announces she is making ensalada de bacalao . . .
and codfish, my friends,
has got a smell that is POWERFUL.

Before I know it
my brain is working fast,
¿me entiendes?
'Cause me? I'm vegetarian.
And Mami? On one of her unnecessary diets.
And Mimi? Now that she's sick, eats like a bird.
And Dad? Ha. I don't think he's been around for dinner
since maybe the night Mimi came home.

Te conozco, bacalao

Mami taught me that saying,
and I ponder it that night
as I plan out my revenge.
They say it a lot in Puerto Rico.
It means: I know what you're up to.
It means: Don't pretend.

But it means that after dinner,
Mami comes and sits on my bed,
because even though she doesn't know about Akiko
I guess she's noticed other things instead.

Creo que deberíamos visitar a la Dra. Salazar,
she says casually,
like she's suggesting a trip to the bookstore
and not Hopkins Child & Psych.
Creo que tu medicina no está funcionando como antes
y una visita no estaría de más.

And I wanna scowl and tell her
how she never LISTENS,
and just because I got in trouble at school
once (twice)
doesn't mean it's all on me.
Doesn't mean it's my meds not working

or my flashbacks coming back.

How every time she asks Dr. Carrot (aka Salazar)

to change my meds,

it means mood swings and not being hungry

and always falling asleep.

That sometimes other people do things too,

and it's not fair

that always

ALWAYS

the spotlight is on ~~mwa~~ moi.

But I know that'll just get me in trouble,

so I count again

fast and soft.

Anyone else would get it,

would read the room.

But Mami? This is always our issue.

She never knows when to stop.

She's all blah blah blah school

and blah blah blah moods,

and finally I just snap:

I am fine!

My medicine is fine!

I've already talked to Dad about the school stuff!

¡PARA YA!

Except when her mouth drops open,

I realize my mistake.

I realize it real fast.

And suddenly

my lungs need more air

than my nose can force down.

I open my mouth

~~to breathe~~

~~to confess~~

but then Mimi calls Mami,

and Mami gives me a look,

and then she's gone and I can panic

and cry it all down.

I'm Not Crazy

I'm not.

And honestly I hate that word. Period.

I go to school.

I start gardens.

I write.

I scrunch my curls with cream

so they look nice every day.

Basically, I'm **OVER** that.

I take my pills 'cause Mami makes me,

not 'cause I still need them.

And Mami would know that

if she ever bothered to ask.

Still.

Mami's face.

I wish I could talk to her.

Really talk. Like we used to.

But there are a lot of things

that aren't the way they used to be,

and Mami and I?

I don't know if we can ever go back.

Smells Like Bacalao in Here

Amir knows it was me right away.

He corners me Thursday at lunch.

Rambling on about promises,

and futures,

all **HOW COULD I**

and trust.

Por favor.

Like this is my first time.

I wore gloves. I did it early.

And as I watch them scrub,

I know nothing is gonna get that smell

out of their lockers.

Not even vinegar and lime.

Amir Doesn't Ride the Bus Today

He walks.
So today, I gulp down all my static-y nerves
and plop down next to Akiko,
who scooches over and smiles.

It was me, I tell her,
and wait for her shocked/proud grin.
Instead, she looks confused.
You what? she says.
And it's almost like time slows
and stills.

Something inside me tells me to stop,
backtrack,
run the other way,
but it's hard to control my tongue
when it has a plan,
when it wants to shout
and share the joy
and celebrate.

The codfish, I whisper.
I'm the one who put it in their lockers.
And finally, her face changes,
but not in the way I thought.
Not in the way I wanted.

Instead of closer, she pulls away.
Instead of gratitude, she rumbles.

You should sit somewhere else,
she says. Firmly. No debate.

And I don't know where I go in my head
but it's not where I'm supposed to—
it's that dark place I have no control in instead.

And next thing I know the bus is parked
and the driver is calling Mami
and every single face but Akiko's is pressed to the window,
watching me stand on the street.

Mami Is Quiet in the Car

I can smell her anger, though.
Like oil that's left frying for too long.

I look out the window,
pull a pencil from my hair,
use it to stab little gray dots
along my knuckles and nails.

Mami slaps it out of my hand
and I glare at her—

¿Qué quieres que diga, Mami?

—because I can tell she is waiting me out,
making me speak first.

Iveliz, ¿qué te pasa? she says.
¿Por qué estás actuando así?

And what irks me about her question is not the
what's wrong,
but the implication that I am acting in some way
that is different, that is abnormal,
that is so far away from who I need to be
as Mami's daughter

that she is just spent

and tired and alone.

I spit at the floor of the car

and Mami grabs my shirt and yanks it,

HARD,

takes her eyes off the road to yell:

¿Te has vuelto loca?

And maybe I have.

Maybe I **am** crazy.

Because when she grabs me?

I'm not in her Toyota, I'm in Dad's Ford.

And when she grabs me?

The entire road around us gets dark

and silent and slow,

until all I can hear is my heart pounding,

all I can feel are shards of glass that are not there

making me bleed invisible drops,

and the only person who would understand

the only person who would know

IS NOT HERE

and so I close my eyes,

feel her let go,

lean my seat all the way back,

and spend the rest of the drive

tuning out what she is saying

and wishing time could turn back.

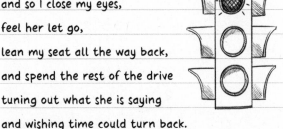

Powerless

Have you ever felt like you're somewhere else, even when your feet are planted firmly in the <u>now</u>? Something not quite like déjà vu and not quite like a nightmare, but something with visions and feelings and sound? I know the word is "flashback" and not "hallucinations." The word is "PTSD" and not "bad." But it doesn't matter how many times Dr. Turnip explained it to Mom, because she's the one who most makes it happen, and she's always the only one who can make it stop.

And me? I'm the one who keeps distracting everyone. I'm the one who gets everyone lost.

Apologies

I think Mami apologized in the car.

She can tell when she triggers me,

even if she also thinks it's kind of stupid

and calls me a dramática

when she thinks I'm

being mañosa just for kicks.

But when she apologizes for real,

when she actually knows what she did,

it means it's too late,

I'm too far

     u

     n

     d

     e

     r

like my head is quicksand

sucking all my organs

in.

I Video Call Amir from My Room

Because by the time we get home,
I feel so small that if I'm not seen
I think I will disappear.

He picks up
(gracias a Dios)
and I immediately start crying.

He waits until I stop.
Quiet.
Just there.
And though I want to tell him about the car
and Mom,
I tell him about Akiko instead.

I tell him I don't know what I did on the bus.
He tells me he does.
That word got around.
He says I screamed and threw my backpack.
That I wouldn't stop yelling,
even when the driver told me to stop.

I could pee myself, I'm so relieved.
I didn't hurt Akiko? I ask.

He shakes his head:

You didn't hurt anybody.

You know you never would.

And he's wrong, of course, because I hurt Dad

and today almost hurt Mom,

and if I can do that wide awake,

how much worse could I be

when all my senses run away?

Malgare, he says,

pressing his fingers to the screen,

repeating what to me sounds like

nonsense Spanish

but I know means "friend,"

"amigo,"

in the Pashto he holds dear.

So I press my fingers to his on the screen

and I breathe.

I didn't hurt anyone.

Malgare.

Amigos.

For real.

What's Going On, Ive?

Amir asks me when I've calmed down,

when we speak again later that night.

What's going on, Ive?

Like I can just snap my fingers

and bust my heart out on the screen.

Like I can just tell him about Dad

coming by more often,

or wanting new friends other than him,

for wanting to feel NORMAL

or trying to love Mimi as she is.

You know you can tell me everything, right?

he says,

and I look at him and I know it's true.

I can, Journal. I can.

But instead of opening my mouth,

I just shrug and watch him deflate,

just a skinny boy and his best friend,

buried deep in her mind.

Malentendida, an Acrostic

Maybe my brain is broken

Akiko and Amir think so, I'm sure

Like how I thought the prank was funny but

Even my best friend and almost friend

Ni siquiera laughed once

Tomorrow is a new day and I know I should

Elevate

Not

Drown, but

I know I'll be going back to ISBI and

Deserve it, I guess, but c'mon

Ayúdenme—don't let me down

I Sit with Mimi After Dinner

Because Mami is angry washing the dishes,

and I don't want to talk to her anyways.

Despite everything she's said, Mimi is **still** better.

Softer.

Lets me lean on her warm shoulder

and cuddle and not talk.

Today she pets my hair and hums,

some Puerto Rican lullaby I can almost remember

if I concentrate,

lyrics I can almost sing

if I wasn't quite who I am.

And I wonder if she knows who I am right now.

If it matters, really, as long as she lets me lean on her,

inhaling her soft grandma smell

that transports me all the way to her house.

I decide it doesn't, so I don't ask.

Instead I say: Mimi, ¿tú me vas a querer siempre?

And she sighs happily and kisses my forehead,

and murmurs something in Spanish that I don't quite catch.

I Used to Be Good at School, You Know

Used to get As and Bs and stickers,
and every teacher (come conference time)
couldn't wait to tell my mom and dad
what a bright light I was.

And maybe I just changed,
or maybe my light was
battery powered and ran out,
but no teacher would ever say nice things now,
and depending on the semester
I'm either just passing
or about to flunk out.

I know people talk about me,
I know they know I know they know
why I missed so much school
and got all turned around.

But I don't know what's worse:

becoming outright invisible
or having everyone watch you
as you slowly fade out.

ISBI, II

I know the principal has it in for me now.
It's not in my head; she told me outright—
all, Ive, I am watching you extra closely now,
so I am working hard,
ignoring the girls cussing at each other behind me
and the boy snoring next to me
when the classroom phone rings
and gets everyone hype.

When Mrs. Silver
(not her name, but look at her hair—it should be)
tells me to grab my stuff 'cause my mom is in the office,
I know it's bad news.

Because if Mami is here,
it means she took off work.
And if she took off work,
it means it's something I'm not gonna like.

And the pizza I had for lunch
is threatening to come up
because I know. I KNOW.

There can only be one reason Mami is here right now.
And it starts with a Dr.
and ends with an -urnip.

Current Seventh-Grade Goals

- ☐ Do what Mami says (the first time she asks)
- ☑ Help Mimi settle in
- ☐ ~~Be more social? Idk~~
- ☑ ~~DON'T GET SENT TO ISBI AGAIN~~
- ☐ Figure out how to grow gandules
- ☑ Be patient with Mimi when I have to repeat myself
- ☐ Do not tell Turnip ANYTHING

Shouldn't *I* Get to Decide?

That's what I ask Mami in the car.
I mean it's my body and my brain—
don't kids have any rights?

O sea, I know I needed the therapy back then,
back when IT happened, Journal,
but that's 'cause I literally wasn't eating
or getting out of bed.

But I'm fine now. FINE.
And Mami had said as long as I took my pills
(dizque to help me sleep and not be sad),
the actual therapy was *my* choice.
That's why we stopped.

But I guess going back on your word
is cool now.
Guess a little ISBI and talks with the principal
are enough to make everyone an embustero,
cómo si how I'm doing in school is somehow
equal to all sorts of other things in life.

Pero total. I should've known.
Dad promised me tons of stuff,
and where is he now?

He Smiles When We Walk In

But I know it's fake.
No doctor—
sorry, *psychologist*—
wants to hear their ex-patients are having "problems."
They want to know we're Tony the Tiger GRRREAT.

And Mami?
Her smile is the biggest and fakest,
making me squirm in my chair
with her how-you-beens
and long-time-no-sees.
And maybe Dr. Turnip can tell,
'cause he asks Mami to leave
real quick.

Do you know why your mom called me?
he says, eyes thoughtful and wide.
Except I know I don't actually have to answer.
Because he will just tell me
so long as I wait him out.

She seems to be under the impression, he continues,
that you're getting into quite a bit of trouble at school.
That you're angrier, and moodier . . .
Pause.
. . . and talking to your dad too?

Eah.

I can't move.
I can't think.

And though I hear Turnip saying:
Hey, what is your brain doing right now? Can you tell me?
Fight, flight, or freeze?
it's like I'm hearing it from outer space.

Iveliz, he says.
Breathe. Count your numbers.
Let's unfreeze your brain.

So I try to focus.
I count squares in the ceiling.
I count blinds.
I count the yellow wisps of dust
floating in front of the window,
until my fingers slowly start to feel mine.

But when my head moves again,
when I feel real and okay and FINE,
I look to my right,
and wouldn't you know it?
Dad has popped in for a visit.
And he smiles, Journal. He **smiles.**

Not Now

You know when you try to mind message
your parents,
and you know they understand you,
clear as day,
and they're just pretending not to?

Dad knows I want him to leave.
He knows it's not the time.
But he just chuckles and leans farther back in the chair,
and if I could punch him out of the room
without Turnip seeing me,
I would.
Wouldn't think twice.

Un poquito

I ignore Dad for now,

and tell Turnip about my list of goals.

See, I know how he works.

I've been here before.

The trick is to say enough

to make him think I buy in,

but not enough

to actually share all my feels.

And surprisingly, he likes the list a lot,

though he says I shouldn't cross stuff out.

That failure is not permanent

and I should be able to try again

as many times as I want.

Which, okay, I guess. Not that I'd ever tell him.

See, sometimes Turnip gives real good advice,

and to be honest, he really helped me out a lot

~before~

but I feel like I'm good now. Good.

And I'm tired of being that girl

who's different

who's special

who went through a "hard time"

and basically messed up her home.

Rules for Surviving Therapy

1. Don't tell Turnip anything you don't want to say.
   You don't need to be fixed, and speaking up always
   leads to people wanting to fix things.

2. Don't listen when he says you're not there to be fixed,
   you're only there to learn "healthy coping skills."
   This is a lie. See rule #1.

3. Do the activities (sensory box, drawing, feelings jar)
   ONLY because you like them anyways and they're chill.

4. Never tell Mami what happens in therapy, especially if
   it has to do with IT.

Three's a Crowd?

Amir and I are eating at our usual spot

(under the trees,

away from the crowds).

He's telling me about his brother,

the littlest one,

who is once again having problems

with his heart.

And I'm listening, sort of,

Journal, I really am,

but when I see Akiko walking toward us,

lunchbox in hand

and mouth stretched in a frown,

my face gets hot and I clench Amir's hand,

pretend to rummage through my backpack for something

anything

to avoid a fight.

I look up,

my stomach a mixture of gas and fire,

and I'm not thinking about Amir

or his brother,

because all I can focus on is

Akiko

and whatever is about to come out

of her mouth.

You can't just get angry at me like that,

she says.

For no reason. When I wasn't even wrong.

I don't like revenge. It's childish. And stupid.

And I definitely don't like other people doing it for me

when I didn't ask.

I am stunned.

Couldn't speak even if I wanted to.

Couldn't defend myself

if I tried.

Finally, Akiko breaks eye contact,

walking halfway to the school's side entrance

before looking back, eyes finding mine.

And for a second? I forget myself.

Cock my head

and smile.

She smiles back.

A little one.

But still.

I might have a chance.

Can I have another friendship?

Can I prove that I can be social

and normal

and fine?

I love Amir, I do,

but sometimes I wonder if he's

the exception—

the only other kid who will ever like me,

and only 'cause he too has seen

some messed-up things in his life.

Gardening Class

School is hard lately,

not gonna lie.

It feels like all my teachers are against me,

assuming I'm playing

faking

when I say I don't understand,

but when stuff happens

(like with Akiko)

it's honestly just too hard for me to care enough

to show up enough

to actually try.

But gardening class?

Literally the best part of my day.

Because Ms. Shannon never gets angry

if I'm unfocused or dazed out,

just finds me something repetitive and calming

to do with my hands.

Turning soil with a little rake

under that partly cloudy Maryland sun?

It makes me feel GOOD and planted

and h-e-r-e,

like

if I stretched

my toes they could

break out of my sneakers

and curl

around the little

worms   and   beetles

I imagine are happily waiting for

the

seeds

we're

about

to grow

Mimi's Garden Is Magic

I can find her tending the deep planter tubs
every day after school,
kneeling on an old yoga mat
she found in Mami's closet,
her soft knees leaving Mimi-sized spots
in the faded rubbery blue.

Today she looks up at me,
grin as wide as anything,
and says my name with such happiness
that I know she sees me.
The Me me
and not a young Mami
or the me I sometimes fake
when I'm at school.

I sit next to her,
finding a spot on the balcony
still warm with afternoon sun,
and watch her fertilize the seedlings
with some coffee grounds from the island,
like the plants will be able to tell
some Café Lareño
from regular old Maxwell House.

Tu papá te estaba buscando,
she says to me,
all calm and matter-of-fact,
like my dad looking for me is something normal,
something that would ever happen—
and she must notice my silence
because she gestures inside.

And I know it's the Alzheimer's, Journal.
I know it 100%.
But my heart is still beating loud and hard
as I slide open the glass door
and head back inside.
Because when Mimi says Dad is here,
well,
what if she's right?

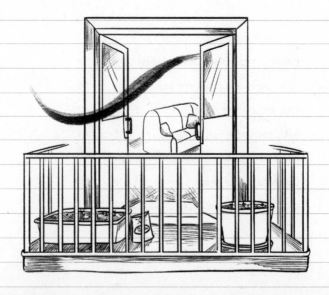

Hide-and-Seek

I start in Mami's room.

(Rapidito,

'cause who knows if she'll pick today

to show up early and ground my butt.)

I check under her bed

and in the closet.

Behind the shower curtain

and the desk.

Pero he's not there, obviously,

so I tiptoe into my own room,

half expecting Dad to jump out from behind the door,

like he used to scare me

back when he was still in the apartment

and everything was good.

My room is empty too, of course,

and then I do get angry,

rabiosa,

for real for real,

and it feels like a whole

flamethrower is inside my chest.

How DARE
Mimi do me like that,
how DARE she make me
all lovesick inside,
and I punch the wall so hard
so many times
my anger turns into crying,
and when Mami finally walks in
(an hour later),
she takes one look at my swollen blue fist
and drops her purse on the ground.

I Tell Mami

Because what else can I do?
She is shaking me and talking,
always talking,
like if she uses the right words,
the right tone,
the right force,
it'll make the truth come crashing out my mouth.

So I tell her what Mimi said,
and the places I looked,

Pero tu papá no está aquí, she says.
Dime que lo entiendes, Iveliz.

And I shrug,
and Mami's eyes are wide,
her face all pale and stretched.
She talks to me in English now,
high and loud like a yelping cat,
like she'll just bust if I don't agree.

Daddy is dead, Iveliz.
He is dead.
Tell me you get it, please.
He is NOT here.

I Go to Bed Without Dinner

I just write and write and write.
Basically these last three pages.
Maybe more? I'm too tired to flip back.

It's stupid how a journal is the only one I can talk to right now.
The only one who won't judge me or call me crazy
or mad.

Because even Amir isn't perfect,
and even if he says he isn't judging,
that's impossible,
because nobody could be that good
in front of my bad.

So who am I left with?
Mami? That's a joke.
Turnip? I'm a job.

And definitely not Mimi,
who pretends to see Dad
but doesn't really,
who says she loves me
but then tells me I'm too good
for therapy,
like maybe she wouldn't care
if I just bled into the ground.

Sangrando

I used to think about that before,

you know.

Hurting myself.

Because some nights I was so lonely

so empty

so NOTHING

that I just wanted to remind myself

I was a real person.

With feelings. And soft skin. And blood.

Pero I never did anything.

Never went past thinking the thoughts.

I guess at the end of the day

I'm just a girl who accidentally hurts others

but who can't bring her hands

to do it to herself.

Throwback Thursday

Two years ago,
during "the dark time,"
Turnip made me make a list.

He gave me a gel pen
and some paper,
and told me to write down ten (10!)
statements that I sometimes forget
but want to remember.

This morning I pull out the list,
smoothing the creases like
it's been no time at all.
Tape it to my jiggly Walmart mirror,
and stare at it until the words get blurry
and my alarm goes off.

Ten Reminders by Iveliz Margarita Snow Medina

1. My dad loved (loves?) me very much.
2. Amir is my best friend.
3. Yo sé hablar dos idiomas.
4. IT was not my fault.
5. I am a good writer.
6. I can tell when something is not real.
7. Nobody is perfect.
8. Mami misses him too.
9. Hurting myself is not going to fix anything.
10. I am not a bad person.

I Find Amir During Lunch

He doesn't look at me,
which means he's still upset,
but I'm not sure if it's because
Akiko interrupted his story
or because I wouldn't answer his questions
after she left.

He doesn't look at me,
but he also doesn't tell me to leave.
So I don't look at him either,
but I also don't leave.

He eats his leek bolanis.
I eat my rice and beans.
We are quiet chewers.
We are quiet people.

I peek at his Tupperware and he half smiles,
offers me some of his spicy okra.
And I half smile back,
scoop some yellowed rice next to his food.

I bite my lip. Start. Stop. Start again.

The words sound loud in my mouth

and I'm not sure exactly why I'm saying them,

but I go ahead anyways:

I'm sorry.

I Explain a Little

How Mami is mad at me for the suspensions.

How I'm failing class.

How last night I was thinking about

                                  when I used to think about

what it would be like to make my arms bleed.

And when I'm done,

when I've told him about school

(if not about Dad or Turnip

or Mimi's chats),

he picks up my hand and squeezes it tight.

You are my best friend,

he says, all slow and sure,

probably because he doesn't know about

all the things I'm keeping secret,

all the things he doesn't know.

But what if I get sent away?

I ask.

Like to one of those residential places

for kids who need help?

And he smiles
and hugs me soft.
If you get sent away,
no matter where,
I will save all my money to come find you.

Then he is serious and looks at me straight:
But you have to be somewhere I can find.
You understand?
Somewhere I can find.

I nod, because I know what he is saying
and what he is not saying.
He can't find me if I'm not here.

Goals List

I think about my goals list during class,
'cause it's better than staring at the board
                        all lost,
and wish what Turnip said about
erasing and starting fresh
could be applied to school (to every class).

I don't even know why I'm
still keeping goals
when the original inspiration
(new grade, new start)
is clearly already a flop.

I mean, who's this list helping?
Because it's certainly not me
or Mami or Mimi or really
anyone at all.

It's hard, being a disappointment,
when everyone around you seems
to be doing just fine.
When being happy is easy for all the other kids,
and their laughter (and grades) in school
is constantly
always
leaving you behind.

Updated Seventh-Grade Goals

- ☐ Do what Mami says (the first time she asks)
- ☑ Help Mimi settle in
- ☐ ~~Be more social? Idk~~
- ☑ ~~DON'T GET SENT TO ICBI AGAIN~~
- ☐ Figure out how to grow gandules
- ☑ Be patient with Mimi when I have to repeat myself
- ☐ Do Not Tell Turnip ANYTHING
- ☐ Tell Amir what is going on in my head when it happens
- ☐ Do not hurt myself no matter what
- ☐ Try again with Akiko

Corazón de melocotón

Amir isn't on the bus again,
and I immediately break out in a cold sweat.
But then Akiko waves me over,
saying,
You can sit here if you're gonna be normal,
smiling, so I know it's a joke.

So I smile too,
because joking is what kids do,
and I tell her that I like her perfume.
'Cause compliments are good for getting people
to like you, I think,
and I guess I'm right,
because she says thank you,
fishes the bottle out of her pack,
shows me the sparkly Victoria's Secret label:
DARING PEACH DAISY
written on the front.

I am frozen but not frozen.
Warm but not warm.
I listen to her talk about some Netflix show
the whole way to my stop,
but right now, Journal? I couldn't tell you
what the heck it was called.

I Find Mimi by the Bus Stop

And at first I think she is waiting for me,

for my bus,

which makes me happy,

because nobody has waited for my bus

since I was maybe seven or eight.

But then I see she is barefoot and in her bata,

and a tingly feeling starts in my belly

and makes my head ache.

Mimi seems relieved to see me,

kissing my cheek over and over,

calling me by Mami's name,

and I grab her hand tight

and look at her in confusion,

because I know my Mimi—

and no earrings or lipstick?

She wouldn't be caught dead.

She tells me she got locked out,

and it seems important to her that I believe her.

I don't know if I do, really,

but who am I to judge?

Maybe Baltimore Mimi

is different from Island Mimi.

Maybe she's doing the American thing
and walking around in pajamas,
pretending they're clothes.

I take her back to our gray building.
Use my key to get us inside.
Grab her some water.
Pour some cereal in a bowl.

Prométeme, she says seriously,
and then I'm nodding,
promising her,
swearing to her.
Vowing I won't tell a soul.

I Should Be Doing Homework

But instead I use my Chromebook to look up dementia.

I want to know. Want to be prepared.

I know some people who have cancer have timelines.

Probably Alzheimer's does too.

But if I ask Mami she'll lie, and

the internet? It always comes through.

And Google knows. It tells me real quick.

Because according to Google,

Mimi is somewhere between stages 4 and 5,

probably closer to 5.

Aka she forgets names sometimes,

but not all times,

and recent things like Dad being gone.

And, like,

Mami helps her with buttons and bra hooks,

but she can garden.

She can eat.

And she definitely goes to the bathroom

all by herself.

And this is good news. Great!

Because stages 5 and 6 last years,

Journal, and so does 7

(though 7 seems too sad).

Which means I don't need to feel guilty
about not telling Mami,

because ¿hablando claro?
This is nothing. Mere stage 5 situation.
Nothing at all.

I Sit with Mimi Before Bed

But when I cuddle up to her,
all she's doing is swiping around on the iPad screen.
It'd be funny if she didn't look so ghostly,
but she does,
so I whisper: Mimi, ¿estás bien?

She smiles at me,
sets the iPad down.

Claro que sí, mi amor. Clears her throat,
gestures at me to wait,
then says slowly, in English:
It was a good day.

I smile at Mimi's accent,
a small gift I rarely ever find,
because Mimi can understand a lot of English,
but she always says she's too self-conscious
to speak it out loud.

She goes back to the iPad and my smile fades.
I want to trust her. I do.
But did she say it was good
'cause she's pretending she didn't get lost
or because she already
doesn't remember she did?

Bribes

Mami is making pancakes when I get up
and I look at her suspiciously,
even as she gestures for me to sit,
like she is a pancake-making type of mom
every day of the week.

Cualquiera diría,
she says laughing,
que nunca te hago desayuno.

But she doesn't, really.
Ever make breakfast.
And jokes always fall flat
when they're true.

One fluffy stack doused in maple syrup later
and she cracks.
Tells me we're going back to Dr. Turnip.
Surprises me, just like last week.
But this time, I know it's not random,
know she's booked him out
in advance.

Adults think kids are so stupid.
We're really not, you know.
We can spot a lie from a mile back.

Therapy

Dr. Turnip wants to talk about Mimi,

about her Alzheimer's,

about "transitions,"

about my life.

But when I grab my rainbow fidget toy

and sit on his couch,

that's not really what comes out.

I ask him why Mimi thinks therapy is bad,

why she thinks my medicines are drugs,

why sometimes I agree with her

even though I don't want to,

I really don't.

Do you think your Mimi,

Turnip asks,

would take medicine to help her Alzheimer's?

I nod, then frown.

Because who wouldn't?

If it was actually a thing.

Yeah, I tell him.

Only problem is it doesn't exist.

You're right, he says. It doesn't.

But there are medicines to help

with other things

just as valid as Mimi's disease.

And I roll my eyes. Because I get it,

sure.

But it still doesn't help me talk to Mimi,

and it doesn't help me feel less hurt

when she says the things she sometimes does.

Turnip reads my mind,

because he always does,

and glances at the door.

Maybe you should talk to your mom about it,

he says,

maybe your mom could help you be a good advocate,

help with Mimi and you.

But I grunt and roll over,

and mutter: next topic,

tell him about the second test

I failed this week at school.

Because asking Mom for help?

No, sir.

Not gonna happen.

Entrometida

On the drive home,

Mami asks how my session went.

All casual, like she really doesn't care,

like she's not peeking over every two minutes

trying to see what I'm doodling,

like it might be about her.

But she always does this, so it's hard to care.

Her whole being present sometimes,

then gone others,

this whole asking questions

but not listening to answers.

So instead of answering,

I tell her about Akiko,

and how I might have a new friend.

And that distracts her enough

that before I know it we're home,

and she's pulling into our building's lot.

Distracts her enough that I'm

halfway out the car door before she remembers

and says, Espera, and grabs my arm.

I stop, because I know what she wants to ask,

even if she's too afraid to say it.

So I yank my arm out of her grasp

and roll my eyes,

throw my doodles back into the car.

I'm not gonna hurt myself,

I tell her,

but if I was,

you're not the one

con quien I would talk.

Iveliz, she starts—

except I'm already halfway across the parking lot,

shoulders rolling back, fake smile on,

ready to see Mimi

and pretend nothing is actually wrong.

Sharing Is Not Caring

This is why there's no point in talking to Turnip. No point
in actually telling him the stuff I told Amir. Because Turnip,
he's been clear. Any hint of self-harm and he'll tell Mami. Any
mention of harming others and he'll tell her as well. Dizque
y que to protect me and others. Y que to keep my well-being
number one. But if Mami already acts this way regularly,
without Turnip tattling and stuff, how would she act if I treated
therapy the way I should?

Solitary

Mimi is in the living room
and she's surprised to see me,
asks where I've been,
but when I tell her therapy,
she makes the kind of disappointed face
that has me walking even faster to my room,
before Mami comes in.

I know Mami thinks she needs to ask
insert eye roll "just to make sure,"
but what she doesn't get is there is
no point in asking
when she's not gonna listen,
and caring doesn't feel as good
when people only do it 'cause you're
too sad, too *you.*

I'm twelve now, almost thirteen,
practically a young adult.
But it's like she somehow thinks Dad's visits
are gonna push me
to lock the bathroom door.

I wish I could tell her

they won't

and have her believe me.

Tell her Dad's visits are new

but not bad,

es que sometimes?

I'm just honestly

too

tired

to

fight

her

back.

Dad Is Here

Which is nice because
he hasn't been coming as often.

'Sup, I say,
and he laughs and sits on my bed,
which I watch carefully for creases and dimples,
any sign
that he might not be 100% dead.

What are you looking at?
he asks,
smile fading,
like he can tell what I wanna know.

Instead, I say:
Why don't you ever visit Mom?
and he sighs a little
and scrunches his mouth,
and I can almost feel the bed creak
under him
as he stretches out his back.

I visit her sometimes, he says.
When she's dreaming.
But I don't think she remembers.
She never opens her eyes.

I'm supposed to know what's real,

I tell him,

and he nods,

his hand brushing mine.

Your poems are real, he says.

And those gandules I saw growing outside.

I stare at him.

¿Y tú?, I ask.

Well, he says,

serious and soft,

with that voice I miss fiercely

every day and every night.

I guess that depends, really.

On what?

On who you ask.

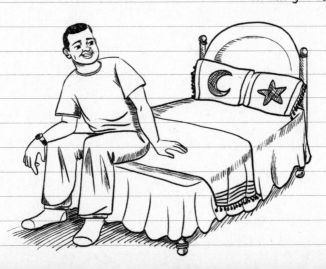

Current Seventh-Grade Goals

- [ ] ~~Do what Mami says (the first time she asks)~~

  Let's be real. Not gonna do this.
- [x] Help Mimi settle in
- [ ] ~~Be more social? Idk~~
- [x] ~~DON'T GET SENT TO ICBI AGAIN~~
- [ ] ~~Figure out how to grow gandules~~ Mimi's got this.
- [x] Be patient with Mimi when I have to repeat myself
- [ ] Do Not Tell Turnip ~~ANYTHING~~ the important things
- [x] Tell Amir what is going on in my head when it happens
- [x] Do not hurt myself no matter what
- [x] Try again with Akiko

Saturday Is for Cleaning

—the house and my hair.

So I use my favorite shampoo,

the one with papaya,

then head over to Mimi

and her spiky aloe vera leaf,

which she slices and strains

until it's a goopy green.

I help her,

smearing green syrup from roots to ends,

letting her detangle even when it hurts,

pretending my teary eyes are from hair pain

and not something else,

something about the way she touches me

so lovingly

that confuses me in ways

I can't quite explain.

Then we wrap my hair up

and clean the apartment—

Fabuloso here and Fabuloso there—

until everything is as shiny

as Mami would have made it

if she wasn't always

always

at work.

Mimi and I Cook

Which really means
she cooks,
and I watch like a starving baby,
practically drooling
at the smell of sofrito
and the beans she's making
in Mami's cast-aluminum pot.

She's humming today
and telling me stories about Grandpa Nuni,
and I feel so happy and warm
I think I might melt.

Te quiero mucho, Mimi,
I tell her,
glad for the word in Spanish
that goes where "love" just cannot.

Y yo a ti,
she tells me,
stirring the pink beans
slowly back and forth.

And I wonder,
is there a word for the opposite
of a panic attack?

Because even though she doesn't understand my therapy,

even though she thinks the pills should stop,

Mimi somehow calms me better than Mami,

better than anyone,

and I wish

I could just carry her everywhere

in my Mimi-sized heart.

Happiness

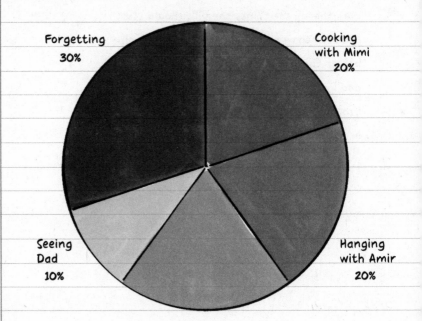

Forgetting
30%

Cooking
with Mimi
20%

Seeing
Dad
10%

Hanging
with Amir
20%

Writing/
Reading
20%

Does Thunder Scare You?

I ask Mimi,
spooning hot rice and beans
into my mouth.

And I think she'll laugh and say no,
already forgetting the other night,
but she actually nods,
mouths the English words,
and says,
"very much."

Y cuando se va la luz, ni se diga,
she adds,
making the sign of the cross.
And I don't press her
but just eat,
wondering if my triggers
are as scary
as important
as thunder
and power outages
and losing access to people
and family
and your house.

Amir's Mom Drops Him Off

Which is new,
because his parents are as strict
as Mami is,
and on weekends Mami is always out.

But now that Mimi is here,
Safeway shifts don't matter,
because there's an adult to watch us
and feed us
and take care of us if we get sick.

Amir agrees to watch *The Baby-Sitters Club* with me,
even though he hasn't read the books,
and we're on the episode where Mary-Anne
wants to paint her room when
I suddenly realize the house is very
very
very
still.

Mimi? I ask.
And Amir pauses Netflix
as we wait for Mimi
to call out or pop in.

Amir, I say.

Help me check the rooms.

Except somehow,

even before we start,

I know Mimi is not here,

she's gone.

Because this is not the first time.

It's the second.

And when I remember my promise,

my lungs go into overtime

and I think I'm gonna puke.

Iveliz. Iveliz.

You stupid, stupid kid.

Why is everything

always

your fault?

Panic Attack

I can tell one is coming

after I check all the rooms,

but I still run out the front door

and down the stairs

like breathing isn't heavy,

like tears aren't already streaming down my face,

like the whole expanse of my vision isn't

slowly shrinking into

                    nothing

                            because

Mimi isn't on the sidewalk

waving to me in her bata,

and she isn't across the road,

laughing at the ugly graffiti

she refuses to call art.

She's not even down the street,

mistaking our building

for its neighbor,

a small thing we could maybe laugh about

later

over tostones and mayoketchup,

hugging after our time apart.

That's when I feel it winning—
the panic.
When I can't see her anywhere in sight.
And when I stumble down,
and Amir yells out,
I can't explain what's wrong
because it's all too much
and I can't move my mouth.

Breathe, he says,
and sits down next to me.
Breathe, he says,
and takes my hand.

And so I close my eyes
and remind myself.
Close my eyes
and forget myself.

Except when the air finally comes back
into my lungs, when I can stand
and **be** and speak,
Mimi is still gone.

She is still gone.
And,
as always,
it's just me.

I Try to Stay Calm

But I can't.

I don't know where Mimi is
or where to even look,
but Amir pulls out his phone
like he's done this before
(maybe he has?),
and when he asks me for my mom's number
I squeak it out in a voice
that sounds very far away
from the girl that I am.

And maybe Mami can sense us
because she answers the phone
even though she's at work,
and Amir tries to pass it to me
but I shove it right back
and shake my head no.

So Amir talks to Mami.
And Mami talks to Amir.
And then he is leading me back
into the apartment,
calling his mom to pick him up,
and telling me to sit still.

Mami Calls the Police

It's what you do,

she says,

when an old person "escapes,"

like Mimi is a prisoner here

and not just in her head,

like Mami owns her body too

and not just mine,

and we all answer to her

because she knows "best."

But when the cops ask her if this has happened before,

when they ask about Mimi's

patterns

and behaviors

and past,

I run into the bathroom and lock the door.

Because I can't.

I cannot lose someone again.

It cannot be my fault.

Por mi culpa, por mi culpa, por mi gran culpa

You know what I'm gonna say,

Dad tells me,

and I nod, because he's told me before,

like a boomerang video that never stops,

playing without me saying a thing.

It's not your fault.

It's not your fault.

It's not your fault.

Except that's a really easy thing

for a ghost to say

and a hard one for a girl to believe.

Because at the end of the day,

I'm here and he's not.

I'm here and Mimi's not.

Mira,

I took fourth-grade math.

I know what a common denominator is.

Soy yo.

The Official Story

It was a Friday, Journal,
and our local bookstore
was having a slam poetry fest,
with poets spitting poems and talking "craft"
and being all the things
I wanted to be.

And my dad didn't want to take me.
It was raining and it was dark.
And he said ten-year-olds had no business
going to poetry nights
where it was gonna be all adults.

But I begged.
And I cried.
Said it was education
and my future life.

And in the end? He said yes.
And in the end? There was a truck.

And when I woke up, I wasn't in the bookstore,
I was in the hospital,
and Dad? Dad was gone.

What Really Went Down

The police? They wrote down there was a truck.

They wrote down how our car slid on some

~~ black ice ~~

but there was no ice

just lying   stupid

adults

'cause my dad didn't slide he ran

and the truck didn't hit us by accident

it hit us when Dad didn't notice that red light—

his eyes on mine

distracted

laughing

all 'cause I was telling a stupid joke

I will never again tell in my whole life.

Onomatopoeia

Roar   Squeal

    Honk   Clang

      Smash   Smack

        Crash

      Buzz   Crack

    Gurgle   Rattle

Hiss   Pop

Mami Has Never Said It

She always refers to it as
"the accident."
And everyone else talks about how
God has mysterious plans.

How it was fate—
how my dad was just too good
too funny
too smart
and so God called him back early
to light up the sky.

Like the whole thing was
una bendición
and not an earth-shattering
catastrophe
caused by a selfish girl
always trying to get what she wants.

But me?
I swear by all that is holy—
I would give up my poems
my people
my life
if only I could bring him back.

Eyes Open / Eyes Closed

When I opened my eyes
I couldn't hear anything,
couldn't see anything.
I didn't know where I was.

Somehow,
I unclicked my seat belt.
Somehow, I crawled out.
Even though people were everywhere,
lights were everywhere,
everyone telling me espérate,
asking me to stop.

And when I saw him,
when I saw his body
and his outstretched hand,
I would love to say I held him,
touched him,
loved him,
but I closed my eyes and screamed,
just screamed,
until I too
fell to the ground.

The Cops Find Mimi

She is sitting at a bus stop three blocks away,
and the cops call Mami 'cause she refuses to move,
refuses to listen,
yells at them in Spanish,
and throws them her shoes.

And when Mimi sees us?
She doesn't look saved or grateful or happy.
She is angry—
angry that Mami sent the cops
when she was just de paseo,
just getting to know her new town.

Angry that she's being treated dizque like a baby
even though she's una mujer
hecha y derecha
(her words)
who was made to move to the mainland
when she really wanted to stay behind.

Mami and I bring her home,
Mami quiet and me quieter,
but it doesn't really matter what we do:
Mimi yells at us the whole way back.

Mami Washes, I Dry

Mimi is in bed.

Mami, I whisper.
And she must sense the humongous secret
I'm about to lay on her,
because she stops washing immediately,
one hand holding the scrubber
and the other this morning's coffee mug.

Mami, no es la primera vez que Mimi se escapa.
I'm so sorry.
Te debí haber dicho. El otro día.
Lo siento.
La encontré enfrente del edificio cuando llegué de la escuela
    y . . .

The kitchen is quiet,
my crying hiccups
and the echo of my Spanish confession of
the details of the day I found Mimi outside
the only sounds bouncing around the sink and countertop and
    stove.

Iveliz, Mami says. No es tu culpa. Mimi está enferma.

And I know Mami is right. That Mimi is sick.

And, like,

I want to believe Mami,

want to believe there's nothing I could have done,

but it just doesn't feel right,

and the words feel forced

on Mami's tongue.

Which is why when Mami makes me promise to tell her

if Mimi ever does anything unsafe again,

I immediately know that

when she said it wasn't my fault, before?

She definitely didn't mean it.

Or she wouldn't have made me promise

to never keep a Mimi secret again.

Language Arts Is Usually My Least Hated Class

But today I am writing in **you** instead.

Real time.

No writing hours later or at night.

Because I wanted to stay home.

Begged Mami to let me.

I just needed the space to

gather myself

and hug Mimi

and thank someone

that everything didn't get all

dark and bad.

That for once one of my mistakes

didn't end up in something

I couldn't take back.

But of course, Mami just said—

Okay, I Messed Up

I messed up so bad
that my hands are shaking as I write this,
as I wait for Mami to leave work and drive
across town,
all to get me when I told her
I TOLD HER
I needed time at home
with Mimi
(and maybe Dad).

I was just writing.
Minding my own business in class.
But I guess that's not allowed
where Jessica is concerned,
because she ripped the journal from my hand so fast
I thought I was dreaming,
and one of my classmates caught it
before I woke up.
I literally just sat there blinking,
listening
as someone
¿quién?
started reading one of my poems,
one of the ones about Mimi and her garden and me.

And then the journal was in someone else's hands,

and I could feel Mrs. Richie in the background,

but my ears were making this buzzing noise

that made it hard to understand.

And I could have maybe survived that,

I think I really truly could have,

except then Justin G. had the journal and

I heard him yell out:

Eyes Open! Eyes Closed!

And then? Then I blacked out.

Mami Doesn't Speak

She doesn't speak when she picks me up
or when the principal tells her I've been suspended suspended—
not ISBI this time, but out of school.
School policy and all,
seeing as how this time,
I actually hit Justin's face.

She doesn't speak when we get home
or when we have dinner
or when I cautiously ask her if I can have Journal back
(though I'm not sure at this point
if I can ever trust you
anymore).

She doesn't even speak when Mimi looks at me
and mumbles under her breath
how it seems she was right and therapy,
it only makes things worse.

Mami doesn't speak
because she never speaks,
and so I take a page out of her book
and shut up too.

Therapy Throwback

Once, after Dad died,
Turnip asked me if Mami and I,
if we ever talked about it
face to face.

If we talked about missing Dad
or being sad
or looking for things to fill time
that before had been his
and not just hers and mine.

And I laughed at him.
Full-on laughed.
'Cause Mami and I aren't talkers,
we're keepers,
holding all our thoughts
way deep inside.

And usually?
I don't mind it.
But sometimes?
Like today?
It gets lonely sitting here
in the dark.

Amir Calls Three Times

But I don't pick up.

I don't know what's wrong with me,
because he is my best friend in the whole world,
and he already told me—
he told me!—
if anyone will still love me it's him.

It's just sometimes I get so deep in my head
it's hard to find my way out.
Sometimes it feels like I can't feel
and everything around me is just swirling about.

I mean, when Justin started reading about Dad?
I wasn't thinking.
I wasn't telling my fingers to fold into a fist,
wasn't telling my mouth to scream.
My body was just doing what it does sometimes
when the world stops wanting to let me in.

So when the computer chimes
and chimes again,
eventually I just snap it shut,

curl up in a ball like I used to do

back when I was little and happy,

and Dad was here,

and Mimi wasn't sick,

and Mami and I didn't feel like we

were oceans

       continents

            planets

                universes

apart.

Bochinche

I tiptoe out to the kitchen to get a snack,

but the light is on in Mami's room

and I can hear her talking on the phone,

her upset whispering

drifting across the apartment hall.

She's talking to one of my aunts in PR,

and even though all I hear is Mami's side,

I get the gist of it real fast:

If I don't start acting more normal—

happier, less angry, qué se yo—

Mami might have to send me to a special school.

The kind of school with therapy every day

and a dorm room

and staff ready to work with special kids

who can't figure out how to fit into

the happy picture of their lives.

And I guess I hadn't realized that my family

talked about me too,

that gossip isn't always the fun kind,

and some bochinche isn't meant to be heard

or—worse yet—understood.

And all of a sudden
I'm not that hungry.

I go back to my room,
rip the Ten Reminders page off my mirror
and then into tiny, tiny pieces that
I flush down the toilet and out
into the sewery goo.

Then I turn the pages back,
black out my seventh-grade goals with Sharpie
and pencil and pen,
and write a new list to follow,
some new rules to help me get through
these endless freaking days.

DON'T

One. **Talk to Dad.** Everyone thinks he makes you worse.

Two. **Fight at school.** Suspension is basically hell.

Three. **Get angry.** You risk ruining your plans.

Four. **Take your journal out.** It might get jacked.

Five. **Share feelings.** Nobody understands.

Six. **Ask for help.** Teachers don't do anything but demand.

Seven. **Let Mimi get hurt.** Always watch the door.

Eight. **Ask Mami questions.** She'll only worry more.

Nine. **Have panic attacks.** They only show you're weak.

Ten. **Cry.** For what? Neither Mami nor Mimi hear you
when you speak.

I Decide to Work on Rule Number Five with Dr. Turnip

Since that's the first place we go the next morning.

Apparently what happened yesterday at school

counts as

"an emergency"

and Turnip pushed our weekly appointment up.

Yippee. Hurray.

Me muero de la emoción.

But you know what they say:

Fake it till you make it.

And so I try. I do.

But Turnip isn't waiting for me to smile,

and he doesn't want to talk about feelings.

Instead he asks about meds.

Specifically, if they're still working.

Um.

I shrug because I don't know what to say.

Are they working?

Honestly, I wouldn't really know.

I've been on them for a while,

since Dad left, I guess,

but I don't usually talk to Turnip about that

since I have a different doctor I see about meds

every three months or so.

Turnip ruffles his notes.

He stretches and looks at me straight.

Says he talked to Dr. Carrot

(aka Salazar),

and Dr. Carrot said I said

(back before school started)

that everything was great.

And I frown because

Dr. Carrot?

Just ugh.

And changing med dosages?

Ugh x two.

Rule number five, Ive,

I remind myself,

because if I can

B-E H-A-P-P-Y,

if I can just stop

with all the messing up,

maybe everything will go back

to how it was before-before.

My meds are working just fine, I say,

and I give Turnip my brightest smile.

And I can tell he doesn't believe me

because he gives me a tiny blue notepad

with little faces and descriptions

of every emotion under the sun.

I won't see you again until next week,

Turnip says.

But I want you to track your moods.

Because sometimes we can't see the patterns

and feelings

until we name them daily,

feel them daily,

and then look back through.

I scrunch my face at the notepad,

because there's no way I'm doing that,

nuh-uh, no way,

but then Mami is in the room

and Turnip is telling her about my assignment,

and I realize I'm going to have to fake the notepad

because Mami's 100% going to check it

every single night.

Por favor.

I'm not nine.

Google Meet

I finally call Amir,

mostly to know what kids are saying

about me punching Justin G.,

but Amir is distant and cold,

and not really how a friend should be.

What is wrong with you?

I finally ask,

because he keeps looking at anything but the screen,

pero his answers are short and unhelpful,

and if I didn't know any better

I'd say Amir was mad at ME.

Amir sighs,

and for a second I don't think he's gonna say anything,

which would be a very Amir thing to do,

but then he looks at me the way I look at Mimi sometimes

and says:

Ive, you haven't been very nice lately.

Really, you haven't even been around at all.

And I am trying to be patient and helpful

because

you are my favorite friend,

but I have stuff going on too.

You call when you want something

and you ignore me when you don't,

and when I try to tell you things sometimes

you don't do a very good job at listening

or remembering

at all.

And Amir keeps talking

but I don't hear anything else,

like my ears got all plugged up

with ocean water

and all I hear is gurgling and waves.

I think he asks if I'm listening,

and I wonder if I can end the call.

I think he asks if I understand,

but my ears are already turned off.

He disconnects,

angrier than when we started,

but, Journal,

I don't even know what he said.

All I heard was:

Ive, you are sick baggage.

What I heard was:

You are a burden to everyone you love.

Real Feelings Journal—Tuesday

In Spanish,

the word "alone" is written

SOLO or SOLA

(or sole/solx),

and it always makes me smile

because inside it,

like a hidden gift,

is the word SOL,

aka sun,

reminding us of what we have

only a letter away in our hearts.

But in English, the word ALONE

sounds like it includes the word

OWN,

and maybe whoever is in charge of

English did that on purpose,

or maybe it was random,

but today it just serves to remind me that

it's my OWN messed-up brain

that made it so I'm always,

no matter what,

alone.

Mimi Is in Her Garden

And I sit with her.

Because it seems like we haven't even talked
since the new rule
where the front door always stays locked
and only Mami and I have the keys.

And so I sit and watch her,
watch her hands pinching off the weeds,
and then she says softly:
Quiero irme a casa, Ive.
Ya ha pasado más de un mes.
I want my home, Ive. Please.

And the longing in her voice
makes my guts twist and turn,
because sometimes I think Mimi and I,
we're not that different,
even if we're two generations apart.

She's trapped in this apartment,
dreaming of a different one
to spread out her stuff,
and I'm trapped in my brain,
wishing for a new one
to stuff all my thoughts.

Being Suspended Is the Worst

But it also kind of isn't.

I don't have to go to school
and pretend I don't have feelings,
or figure out what to do about Amir,
or even Akiko,
who, honestly,
probably already forgot about me.

And I definitely don't have to deal
with gossip or hard classes
or Jessica and Justin G.,
who I'm sure by now
have made me out to be
some kind of hard-core violent beast.

Instead, Mimi shows me how to make her arepas,
and we spend all morning kneading
flour and coconut milk,
making little balls of dough
and frying them golden brown and hot
till they're ready to eat.

We save some for Mami, of course,
but she's at work and arepas taste best fresh,

so Mimi and I chomp on all the rest,

hers stuffed with picadillo

and mine with the soy crumbles

Mami sometimes gets me as a treat.

And when Mimi calls me Tania?

I honestly just let it go.

Because how much must she love me

to call me by a name she herself picked out

almost forty years ago?

Feelings Notepad—Wednesday

Mood: Happy

Why: I made arepas with Mimi and ate so much!!!!!

Dad Ruins It (aka Real Feelings Journal—Wednesday)

He ruins it,

visiting me and Mimi as we lie on the couch,

bellies full of food,

eyes heavy with afternoon sleep.

He winks at me,

sniffs the air,

pops an arepa in his mouth

so fast

that I can't

not

believe.

I look at Mimi,

but she is focused on the TV.

So I remind myself of my rules,

whisper GO AWAY,

and blink so hard and fast

my eyeballs hurt.

Except Mimi hears me and turns,

first toward me, then toward Dad,

and she looks so confused that

I don't even think,

don't even plan,

Just say: Esto es lo que te traté de decir

el otro día. Él me visita.

And I want him to stop.

When she looks at me, though,

I realize my mistake,

because her confusion was not

because she was seeing Dad

(like I thought)

for the very first time,

but because she didn't know who

I was talking to

and was trying to figure it out.

Not that it's a secret, I guess,

at least not from Mami,

but I need Mimi to keep thinking I'm okay.

Can't have her knowing about Dad

(on top of the therapy and medicine)

or she might abandon me and run away.

Although I guess if she thinks I talk to ghosts

she might understand my therapy a bit more.

Pros and cons, Journal.

Pros and cons.

Real Friends Joke Around

I need more friends,
especially if Amir is going to keep being
AMIR,
who I am apparently terrible to
and don't listen to
or whatever he said on that call.

So when I see that Akiko happens to be online today,
her Google Chat bubble all green,
I send her a funny YouTube video link,
just to see if I sink or swim.

Ah, crazy girl is back, she types.
Heard you punched someone.
Anyone tell you, you have anger issues?

I am momentarily stunned
and want to put the computer away,
but then I send her a tears-out-laughing emoji
and the monkey covering his eyes,
and think
this is a normal friendship,
and I swallow everything else back down.

Mimi's Letters

When I come out of my room,
I see Mimi at the kitchen table
with dozens of Grandpa Nuni's letters
(from when he was deployed)
spread about.

And they're VERY romantic,
so much that I kind of want to puke,
but Mimi just laughs and then gets serious,
and she tells me she reads them
once a week
so she doesn't forget.

And I don't know why that trips me up,
but it does,
because for some reason
I kind of imagined that Mimi didn't know
what was going on.
Like that quote Mami keeps on the fridge,
the one that says:
You Don't Know What You Don't Know.

But if she DOES know,
if she knows she forgets,
how must that make her feel?

To know things aren't great in her mind
and they're only going to get worse?

Ay, Ive, ya. No te pongas triste, she says,
because she must have seen my face.
Amar y olvidar no es tan malo.
A veces lo duro es recordar.

Mimi hands me a letter,
asks me how I make sure
to remember my dad.

And I think it's the first time
I've ever heard her
actually talk of him
like he's not
coming back.

And then my eyes do tear up a bit,
because what she is scared of? Forgetting?
Forgetting is what I wish for at night.

Like if somebody offered me permanent memory loss?
Today? Just like that?
I'd probably say yes.
I'd probably say yes, all right?

Open Conversations

That's what Turnip says Mom and I need to have.
He says grieving side by side
is not the same as grieving together,
and sharing a loss is not sharing
if we don't ever talk.

But it's not like anyone else in my family talks either!
Mimi and me? We talk, but not about that.
And Mami and Mimi? I'm no psychic but I can guess,
'cause Mami just isn't like that.

In the past? When I've tried?
It really hasn't felt like she's heard me,
not even a little bit,
not at all.

Question I'll Never Ask Mami

Who would you have chosen to die?

    a) Dad

    b) Ive

Feelings Notepad—Thursday

Mood: Excited
Why: I think I am making a new friend named Akiko.

Real Feelings Journal—Thursday

I almost texted Amir today,
since Mami gave me back my phone.
Honestly,
it would have been so easy,
so freaking easy,
to just write I'm sorry—
PERDÓN.

Except then
I would have to explain my silence
and listen
and share.
And right now?
I couldn't even share my name with someone,
much less my brain.

And listen to him complain how
I'm not good enough?

Just 'cause I have other stuff on my mind
that is not him?
No, no thank you.

It's like I don't even know who I am anymore,
and the more pages in this journal I pass,
the closer the Ive from page one is becoming
someone I don't recognize at all.

Online to IRL?

The school is MAP testing today,
which they apparently don't care if I miss,
and Akiko must have finished early
because she messages me from her computer
complaining of being tired of sitting still.

Akiko seems happy to chat with me,
even invites me to her house.
So I don't correct her when she shortens my name to
Liz (like in Lizard),
and when she mentions doing my hair
I just smile.

Don't worry, my crazy friend,
she says,
I was you once too.
But I've decided you're gonna be my project,
and with this awesome makeover?
I promise—
For real, for real, I'm gonna help you.

And even though now, in bed,
writing those words on paper makes me twitch a little,
I'm still just so freaking happy
that she said the words
"my FRIEND."

Mami Sits Me Down

And it's weird,
because even though I give her my
(fake)
feelings notepad every night,
we haven't really talked much lately,
so sitting on the couch together
like everything is normal and how it used to be
makes the hair on my arms prickle
just a tiny bit.

But then Mami looks at me
the way she looks at the piles of dishes
after a long, long night,
and before I can get ready
or prepare,
she literally clenches her hands
and starts to cry.

Dime, Iveliz, she cries.
¿Dónde fallé? ¿Qué hice mal?
Tu papá sabría que hacer pero yo—

And I don't stay to hear the rest,
jumping off the couch
and dashing into my room.

Before she can list all the ways I've

disappointed—

all the ways,

as she put it,

SHE's failed

to fix me up good.

Feelings Notepad—Friday

Mood: Sleepy

Why: I am very tired but overall had a good day.

Real Feelings Journal—Friday

When Dad died
Mami lost it.
Like she for real, for real lost it,
so much so that three of my titis
came up from Puerto Rico
and stayed with us for a whole two weeks.

All these different women
with their different perfumes
and too-loud voices,
packing me lunches
and washing Mami's hair,
and probably paying for things too,
because I don't think Mami did anything but sleep
for months.

She fell apart
and was ALLOWED to,
and nobody batted an eye when
she stopped going to work
or going out with friends.
Because that's what happens
when you're sad,
that's what's normal
when something happens
that is capital-B Bad.

Sike!

That's what happens

when you're an *adult* and sad.

Because, me? I had to go to school.

And me? I had to eat all my meals.

And sure, everyone talked about how

~resilient~ I was . . .

but is it surviving

when it's other people holding you up?

Mami fell apart back then. And yet now?

She's just fine and great.

And I am falling apart all over again.

Or for the first time.

And I don't know where to turn.

Mami Drives Me to Akiko's

She says she probably shouldn't
'cause of my suspension,
but she thinks I've done my time.
And I can tell this is her way of saying
lo siento
without actually saying the words out loud.

I ask her who will watch Mimi during her shift today,
but she looks at me funny
and says Mimi will be fine.
That she'll watch *Sábado Gigante* reruns,
and either way the door will be locked tight.

That stops the guilty feelings a little bit
but not a whole, whole lot,
and I don't know why I'm so nervous
as Mami pulls up,
but I actually hesitate and my heart speeds up.

And for a second I think of telling her things:
Like how badly I want to start fresh.
How I love Amir but sometimes
I just also wish for more friends.
And also how Akiko confuses me,
sometimes by how she acts,
sometimes 'cause of what she says.

In the end,

I don't say anything.

I'm Ive. It's fine.

I just grab my bag

and kiss Mami

and wave goodbye.

No es no

And I know this. I do.

Pero es que my tongue doesn't work
sometimes
around Akiko,
and so when she plucks my eyebrows
so they're skinny and defined,
I don't say a word,
and when she straightens my curly hair
so it's long and burnt on my back,
I try to smile as big as her,
because she is saying I am pretty
and her mom is saying I am pretty,
and even though I've never really
cared about that before,
maybe pretty is what I want?
Maybe pretty is what she sees?

I'm so lost in my own head sometimes
that I don't even know
what I want to be.

Mami Doesn't Insult Me

When she picks me up.
But she gasps
and an ay Dios mío escapes her lips.
And I know right then that she hates it,
and although I know it's irrational,
I think maybe she also hates me.

But her gasp also makes me angry,
because it's my body, not hers,
and I should get to decide some stuff
like what I eat or
how my hair is gonna be.

I don't say that, though,
just get in the car, silent as can be.
'Cause this new round of rules is working.
I'm fitting in and not messing up (maybe?).
I just gotta trust the process
of my backup plan D.

Feelings Notepad—Saturday

Mood: Brave

Why: I got a makeover! New day, new me.

Real Feelings Journal—Saturday

I stand in front of my Walmart mirror
and try to figure out if I like the reflection,
this girl who no longer has
what people call "pelo malo"
or bushy eyebrows,
this girl who apparently looks cool and pretty
and like she could maybe fit in.

My hair sits heavy on my back,
thick
but in a nice straight way.
Like how I can now use my fingers as a comb
and not need half an aisle's worth
of beauty products
to make it through a frizz-free day.

I smile a little, strike a pose,
examine myself,
feeling like the kind of girl who would never
hit a kid in school or let Mimi escape,
the kind of girl who aces all her classes,
and has friends,
and a dad who speaks to her in voices
that other people
can hear.

On Sunday I Garden

Except the gandules aren't looking too good,
and Mimi seems frustrated and tired.

Te vas a arrepentir,
she tells me at one point.
¿Eso es lo que te meten en la cabeza en terapia?
Tanta belleza natural . . .

And I don't dignify her with an answer,
because therapy has *nothing* to do with my makeover,
and I already know what she and Mami think:
that I'm ashamed of the way I look
and where I come from,
that I am trying to fit in.

Pero really? That's not it at all.
Did I want to say no to Akiko?
Maybe.
Maybe not.
But how do you explain to your family
that it's not that you're ashamed,
but that you're lost?

That sometimes you look in the mirror
and it's so foggy
you just gotta shake it up?

When Amir Video Calls

I make sure I am wearing a hoodie.

He knows what's up, though.

He always does.

And I feel so far away from him anyways

that I want to at least give him

something.

A crumb.

A virtual hug.

So I pull the hoodie off,

let him see my hair and eyebrows

and scared face,

and when I finally open my eyes,

he says:

New day, new you, huh?

And it's like all this weight

lifting off my shoulders and flying off

because finally,

even if I am baggage,

MAYBE

someone gets it—

someone sees me searching

and thinks it's okay.

We Don't Really Apologize

We just kind of . . . move on?

And I mean to ask Amir about his brother,

since that's what he was talking about

the day Akiko showed up,

but I get distracted with

homework questions

and school gossip

and before I know it . . .

we've hung up.

Real Feelings Journal—Sunday

Dad visits after dinner and I ignore him—
pretend I'm doing math,
mumbling equations out loud
so I don't have to hear his

                                    Ive, ven acá.

                      But when he reaches out
                         and touches my hair,
                                I look up,
                 and the sadness in his face is so real,
                              so harsh.
                          He is talking,
           but I can't tell if it's to me or to himself,
        saying how every day I'm going to keep changing
                         and growing
                         and it's his job
                     to not hold me back.

And suddenly my lungs are ice cold,
my dad's reaction
a stunned slap,
and the need to look like ME,
like HIS,
is so strong and terrifying
that I ignore Dad,
don't even say goodbye.

And before I know it

I am sitting in the bathtub,

clothes and all,

trying to wash away both

the sticky dread

and my straight hair

with the hottest water I can stand.

This Morning

Mami almost spits out her coffee
when I come out of my room.
I ignore her,
making my morning toast like
I didn't undo hours of makeover work last night,
like I didn't go to bed with hair wet and tangled
and try to fix it this morning
by forcing it into a frizzy braid.

And before I can help it
my insides start buzzing like
a thousand bees
a hundred crickets
have somehow made a home
in my stupid guts.

Because I know Akiko will be mad,
but maybe I can explain it away.
Say it was an accident,
a flash flood,
anything
that will allow me
to keep my new friend.

Akiko and I, an Acrostic

A selfie sent to her at lunch

Knowing it would be bad

Ignoring the desire to hide

Kinda cursed, it seems, to always make her mad

Or at least that's how it seems

And how can I explain?

No words would do it. So I type

¡DEJAME QUIETA!

I see her start typing. Stop. Start. Stop.

I am alone.

It's Hard to Know What I Feel

I'm _ _ _ _ _ _ _ with myself,
because even though the makeover looked cute,
I ruined it.

I'm _ _ _ _ _ _ _ at Akiko,
because she never asked if I wanted to change,
just assumed I couldn't possibly
want to stay the way I was.

I'm _ _ _ _ _ _ _ at myself,
because if I wasn't sure,
then I should have said no.
But also if I liked it,
I shouldn't have let Mami and Mimi and Dad
get to me, and shame me
into going back to how I was.

But mostly?
I'm _ _ _ _ _ _ _ at Akiko,
for not understanding the things I want to say
but don't,
for being like Amir,
and not being a friend who is perfect
and uncracked,

my opposite in every way.

Feelings Notepad—Monday

Mood: Peaceful

Why: Suspension is honestly not that bad.

Real Feelings Journal—Monday

I video chat Amir that I am done trying to make friends.

That he is enough for me

and now I know what I want.

And he smiles, but it's his sad one,

that one he uses when he talks about

his grandpa Irfan.

And he tells me that friends are good

in theory,

but not always,

and it's important to think

about what we get

but also what we give out.

I think about that,

because Amir is the smartest boy I know,

but the more I think, the more

the darkness swirls.

O sea, is he talking about me and Akiko
or me and him?

Because what it sounds like he is saying is:
Iveliz Snow, you are not okay.
What it sounds like is:
Iveliz Snow, why am I your friend?
What it sounds like is:
Iveliz Snow: I am not happy with what I give
and I'm definitely not happy with what I get.

Dr. Turnip Reads My Feelings Notepad

The fake one,

obviously,

not the one in my journal.

He reads silently,

and quickly,

and then he looks up

and I know I've been caught.

It sounds like you had a great week,

he says.

And I nod.

But is that all that happened?

In your brain?

And I am planning on fully lying,

I have my story all planned,

but suddenly Dad is sitting next to me,

and I get so angry that he's there,

so frustrated at the fact

that no matter how hard I try,

how hard I fake,

Amir still hates me

and Mami would rather have Dad

and Mimi doesn't understand me

and Akiko is just bad,

that all I can manage is

a shrug

before I start to cry.

Turnip Watches Me

And I try to remember
if I've ever cried in front of him before.
Because when I think back,
when I try to picture it in my head,
I don't think I ever have.

Iveliz,
he says,
and I'm struck by how perfectly
he pronounces my name.

Iveliz,
you are not alone.
I don't know what you are going through,
and your mom doesn't either,
and I'm guessing neither do your friends.
But we are HERE. Let us help you.
Let us listen.

And I look at him,
because I don't believe him,
not just yet,

because people love to say they're there for you,

that they know your address by heart,

but then when you need them,

when your heart calls and calls and calls,

they're suddenly nowhere to be found.

Ive, he says.

I know I stopped seeing you before.

Because you wanted to stop.

Because your mom wanted to stop.

Because everyone wanted to move on.

But remember how we asked you to stay on the pills?

Now is your time, Ive.

Because if they're no longer working,

or if you need to talk things out,

now is your moment.

I need you to SPEAK UP.

Frozen

Have you ever wanted
to be someone else?

In that moment,
when Turnip asks me to tell him,
I wish more than anything
that I was the kind of girl who could.

I wish it was possible for me to be happy.
I wish it was possible for me to change.

But if fate and God are the ones who took away my dad,
they're also the ones who injected me
with all this black nothingness.
And no matter how many flashlights I shine,
no matter how hard I try,
I just can't seem to find my way out.

I Try, Though

I really do try.

And so although I don't tell Turnip

EVERYTHING

or even MOST things,

I break my rules a little

and share something that's

been on my mind.

How come I'm supposed to hold it together,

I ask him,

but everyone else gets to fall apart?

How come I *need* to get better

while everyone else gets to chill

and figure it out?

Is that how you feel, Iveliz?

Turnip asks.

Like nobody is giving you space to

feel

and be sad

and engage with your past,

so you have to fight them back?

And I shrug,

because even when I say things

I don't really know what comes out of my mouth,

but Turnip nods and sits back,

and tells me:

Ive, with me?

There are no expectations.

You can fall.

You can let it all out.

And I look at him,

because he's supposed to help me be safe,

but falling? Letting things out?

How can I do that

if I don't know how to get back up?

Failures

Lately it feels like no matter what list

I make or craft,

what rules I decide are important

and will help me not ruin my life,

I keep not following them

I keep not seeing them

I keep not doing them

even though I know   I KNOW

I'm setting my own self up.

And I used to think I was doing better,

I thought seventh grade was gonna be my year,

no doubt,

but maybe I'm not actually doing as okay as I thought,

or else wouldn't it be easier

to sort everything out?

Would You Take Medicine for Your Alzheimer's?

I ask Mimi in Spanish that afternoon.
Because the truth is
it's been bothering me
ever since Dr. Turnip asked me
what I thought Mimi would do.

And Mimi smiles sadly
and says: Si tan solo eso existiera . . .
And I don't wanna start something,
I don't,
but it bothers me that Turnip was right,
and Mimi can't see the sameness
between her imaginary pills and mine.

Why is it that the one adult in my life who is "supportive"
(my mom)
is the one who doesn't hug me or laugh,
while the one who actually holds me
(my grandma)
doesn't believe in the meds
and the therapy
that Turnip says save lives?

Medicine, an Acrostic

Medicine is weird in that

Everybody takes it no problem for a headache,

Diarrhea, or a cold, but

If someone needs it for their sadness

Chaos erupts.

I am trying to not be ashamed but

Not gonna lie, it's hard when it's your own grandma

Even if she has Alzheimer's. Especially when her frown burns

    your heart.

How Is Amir's Brother?

Mami asks after dinner
And I stare at her,
plate and dish towel in hand,
because I literally have no idea
what she is talking about
or why she is starting to frown.

¿Ustedes se pelearon? she asks.
And I shrug,
because I don't actually think
Amir and I are fighting,
but maybe I'm just scared to admit it,
the same way I've been too chicken
to take my pills in front of Mimi,
and keep doing it in secret
just to avoid the talk.

Mami squints at me.
Washes a plate.
Is silent while she washes one more.
His brother is in the hospital again,
she finally says,
and I bet he'd really appreciate it
if you gave him a call.

How I Could Start My Call to Amir

~~Hey, Amir, what's up? Yeah, I know it's been a while . . .~~

~~Amir! Sorry I didn't listen that one day. Is that what~~
  ~~you were . . .~~

~~Amir? How are you, my bff?~~

~~Amir, why didn't you say anything last time we talked?~~

~~Hey, Amir, my mom told me . . .~~

~~Heeeeeyoooooo~~

I Don't Call Him, Of Course

Why would I?
He would know I'm only calling
'cause I found out.

Stupid. Stupid. Stupid.

How is it that I always find a way
to mess stuff up?

Dinner Is Weird Tonight, II

Dad is on the couch,

and I'm trying real hard to ignore him,

but Mami can tell something is up.

¿Por qué no me hablas, Ive?

she asks me,

reaching out to touch my hand.

And even though things with Turnip

turned out okay when I (slightly) opened my mouth,

I don't think that would happen with Mami,

especially after how she acted

the other night on the couch.

And I don't want to tell her

that the reason I don't tell her stuff

(like how her daughter is a terrible friend)

is because despite it all,

despite how we've drifted,

I still can't stand disappointing her

for the thousandth time.

Do You Even Get It, Journal?

Do you understand how bad I am?

I killed my dad.

I almost got Mimi hurt.

I abandoned Amir.

And all Mami asks of me is that I behave

in school,

that I get good grades,

that I help around the house,

and I can't even manage that.

How do other kids do it?

How do they know how to focus

and be normal and fine?

Am I just not meant to be here?

Because every day it becomes harder

and harder

not to take that car crash

as some sort of

cosmic sign.

After Dinner I Go to Take My Pills

Except when I open the cupboard,

they're not there.

Mami, I yell,

did you move my pills?

Busca bien, she yells back,

so I start pulling out bottles of Tylenol

and Pepto Bismol,

and the albuterol

for when I get sick,

like somehow my pills

got magically shifted

and I'll see the little orange containers

hiding behind the Imodium

or alcoholado

or Vicks.

I empty out the whole shelf of meds,

panicking as I move them around,

and when Mami comes in to help me search,

she scrunches up her face

and starts opening random cupboard doors

and peering inside.

Mimi comes to see what the noise is about,

and I turn to her, my face hot and mad.

Mimi, ¿qué hiciste?

And Mimi looks at me, confused—

¿Tania? she asks.

I take a step toward her,

my mind angry and swirling,

but Mami steps in front of Mimi,

her face serious and blank,

and talks to me low and in English,

to try to keep Mimi out.

Listen, Ive. Mimi is not having a good day.

Maybe she moved them and forgot.

We'll find them.

But you can't go accusing—

STOP, I yell at her.

Stop defending her all the time!

Mimi didn't move them "accidentally."

She didn't pick out MY bottles just by chance.

She probably threw them away.

Threw them away on purpose,

all sneaky and knowing and fast!

And even though Mami stares at me

and tells me to lower my voice,

I continue:

Mami,

you KNOW her.

She hates my pills and she hates the therapy I try.

I'm just this awful messed-up daughter and granddaughter

and I wish Dad had lived

and I had died!

Oh is THAT what you wish?!

Mami yells back,

her face so angry

I can't handle it,

making me turn so I no longer hear her voice.

I run to the trash, barely registering her

as she moves a confused Mimi out of the room,

feeling my eyes tear up

as I find all my little pills

sitting in the gunk of the trash-can pile.

I see Mami come back in,

I see her mouth moving into words,

but all I can feel is my blood rushing through me,

my heart pumping hot anger

inside and out.

I kick the can, hard,

and all the trash and pills

go sprawling out over the kitchen floor,

and when Mami yells at me to go to my room,

I tell her I hate her,

I hate me,

and I lock the bathroom door.

Why Did I Survive?

I crumple to the floor,

my crying coming on heavy and hot,

my brain beyond help,

and for once I can't remember my reasons

for not wanting to hurt myself.

Iveliz,

I hear Mami call from the hallway.

Abre la puerta.

Abre la puerta YA.

But I ignore her,

the floor cold against my cheek,

my vision cloudy and half black

as I study the drawers probably full

of small scissors and clippers and razors,

how maybe just maybe

I've been wrong in even thinking

I could ever do the right things.

And Mami? She starts pounding on the door

and jiggling the knob,

yelling how she's gonna get the door open

whether I like it or not.

But right now?

I don't care about Mami,

constantly thinking she knows best,

or Mimi,

who thinks less of me

just because I need help,

or Amir, who I failed

when he needed me most,

or even Dad,

who is always butting in

and yet today

doesn't care enough to show up.

Because all of them?

All of them all of them ALL?

They pretend like they care and want me,

this girl who tries to fit into all these roles—

hija, nieta, amiga—

but really? They'd be much happier

if I was gone.

Iveliz, breathe,

I hear in Turnip's voice.

Iveliz, not your fault,

I hear in Dad's.

Iveliz, espera,

Mami's creeps in.

But I don't listen

because I don't care.

Except just as I sit up

softly

slowly

eyeing the drawer knobs,

the doorknob clatters to the ground next to me,

and Mami busts into the bathroom,

screwdriver in hand,

grabs me by the armpits,

and yanks me up.

The ER Is Busy

So we wait:
me writing in my notebook,
and Mami texting with whoever she got
to look after Mimi
while she drove me here tonight.

It isn't the first time we've been here,
but it's definitely been a while,
and I zone out a bit while Mami talks to a nurse,
tells her how I was thinking about hurting myself
and wouldn't answer her
when she asked me if I was really going to
or not.

It's so stupid, because really, I should have just said no.
I know the drill. Everyone does.
If I say yes or I say maybe
or I don't answer,
Mami will drag me here,
and we'll spend hours and hours waiting
until the doctors clear me to be safe,
until they clear me to go back.

Pero no sé. When she asked me?

My brain was too sad

too mad

too frustrated to talk,

and now I'm here,

and the nurse is asking me questions,

and I guess I should stop writing

and answer

so they'll leave me alone.

Dr. Turnip Shows Up and I Glare at Him

Why are YOU here? I ask,

and he laughs.

I work for the hospital too, he says.

And when they saw you were my patient

they called.

I cross my arms over my chest,

still mad at the thin gown they made me wear,

at the stubby little-kid pencil they gave me to write with,

saying mine was too sharp.

What happened, Ive? he asks.

Remember our last talk?

It's okay to let it all out.

I've said it before and I'll say it again:

I can help you with some coping mechanisms,

I can help you process and talk,

but only you can take that first step.

Only you can decide to act.

And I think about keeping quiet,

about making Mami wait forever out in the hall,

but the anger has leaked out of me by now,

the desire to hurt a memory,

and all I want is to be in my own bed

sleeping all night.

If I tell you, can I go home? I ask him,

and I hate how small I sound.

How weak.

And childish.

And scared.

If I think you and your mom can keep you safe,

Turnip says,

and you promise to tell an adult if it gets bad,

then yes,

you can go home.

And I think about that.

Think of the cold hospital room

and my bathroom floor

and my stomach all on fire,

and then I nod.

I nod,

and I start to talk.

Word Vomit

i don't know why things are so hard now when everything
happened such a long time ago. it was bad yeah but then i was
fine and i don't know why all of a sudden i'm not. mami says it's
'cause i'm seeing dad and i get it i guess but it's not just dad i
don't care what mami says. it's also mimi mi mimi because how
can i love her through her alzheimer's but she can't manage to
love me back? and i know what mami says that mimi loves me
and it's just how she grew up but that's a messed-up reason not
to change when it's your own nieta by your side. 'cause mimi? she
says things like it's all a joke and i'm too soft and can't let it go.
but i am soft **i am** i'm not like dad all big and strong. and i can't
get over how mami takes her side when mimi is the one who is
wrong. how can i deal with all the stuff with amir and akiko and
stupid jessica and justin g. when i can't even be happy at home?
school is so bad it's even worse than it was before. i'm basically
flunking every class and it feels like my teachers have just given
up. plus these kids are always messing with me for no real reason
and they know how to push my buttons so i'll get all angry and
mess up. and amir usually kept me steady every year this whole
time but now he always seems to want more from me and i
never used to think i was a bad friend until now. i'm not good
about thinking about other people or at least that's what amir
said one of the last few times we talked. and when stuff happens
like the fight with akiko or the awkwardness with amir i run
because i just don't wanna talk. but it builds up and up and up
and up and you're so right IT BUILDS UP. and how am i supposed

to get out of bed and pretend to be normal when sometimes
i feel like i'm floating so far out in space there's no point in
having hope? i think mami thinks what happened today was
random, like mimi just pushed me over the edge. that i wouldn't
answer her questions about what i was doing to be difficult to
be a burden when i've actually been thinking about it more and
more with each passing day. i don't want to hurt myself, dr. alex,
i really truly don't. i'm not saying that just so you'll let me go
home es que i think i need help i think I need **you** i just don't
know how to get out of this hole

We Talk

We talk.

We talk and

we talk and

      we TALK.

About Dad and about Mimi

and what healthy relationships

sound like

look like

feel like

to us.

And my homework

(which he says he'll help me with)

is both terrifying and small,

because he says I need to start talking to

~everyone~

family included

so I can decide who is a good fit for my circle,

who will help me move forward

and who is not.

On the Drive Home, Mami Is Quiet

Except this time I know why.
Because after I told Dr. Alex
(feels weird to call him Turnip now
after all that),
he talked to my mom.
And now Mami knows everything
—how truly bad it is in my head—

And I get it.
It's the rule.
But sometimes I wish I was an adult
and the only one in charge of my life.

Don't get me wrong.
I don't regret it, our talk.
I hate Mami knowing, yes,
but it did feel good to finally tell someone
(even if it was a doctor)
just how sad I've been.
How some days I can barely
get through breakfast or walk.
How sometimes Dad won't leave me alone,
but then when I need him,
he's gone.
And how much it upset me,
hurt me,

to have Mimi throw all my pills

out.

Because Dr. Alex? He didn't act like I was crazy,

not at all. Instead he told me about

all the hundreds and hundreds of kids

who see their people after they die.

How it's not my brain being messed up,

but more my heart being hurt,

and how sometimes we think we're okay,

we think we've moved on,

but then our hearts crack open

months

or even years

later

and it's important to stop,

be kind to ourselves,

and ask for help—

ask for love.

Confession

I am not okay, Journal.
Or I am, sometimes,
but most days? I can't wait to go to sleep.
School is an utter mess,
un rebulú total,
and if I manage not to fail a single class
other than gardening
I will count that as a win.

I am not okay,
because I used to be able to talk to Mami,
and Mimi, and Amir,
but now I only talk through my pen,
and a pen can't hold you
when you cry,
it can't love you
until you're fine,
and it definitely can't help you cross out
the things you're done with
in your life.

I am not okay,
because I still see Dad,
and I can't tell anymore
if he's real or not,
if it's a hallucination or magic,

and maybe if he visited me in church
everyone would understand it better,
but he doesn't,
and I'm scared,
because I don't want to get sent away.

I am not okay,
and sometimes
I wish people wouldn't believe me
when I say I am.
I wish they would ask, just one more time,
and I wish they wouldn't tiptoe around me
like I'm a poem,
so I could show them that I'm a real girl,
accidentally cracked.

After Dinner

I make a big deal out of
taking my pills from their kitchen cupboard
and gargling them noisily
next to where Mimi
stands washing the pots.

Mami has explained to me already
how lots of people,
but especially old people,
and especially old people from the island,
don't believe in therapy or prescriptions,
as if therapy was something to be ashamed of,
as if medicine was a secret to be kept.

But I'm not hiding from Mimi anymore.
Because if there's one thing
I learned from Dr. Alex it's this:
the people who want to be with me
will be with me—
no changes required.

Mami, a Confrontation

Podrías defenderme más,
I tell Mami before bedtime,
as I'm leaving the bathroom
while she's coming in.
I mean she threw away my PILLS
and yet you're *still* on her side,
how do you think that makes me feel?

And her mouth drops open,
probably in shock,
but it's not fair that Mami forgives Mimi everything
just 'cause of her Alzheimer's,
when she could be backing me up.

Mimi está viejita,
she starts to say,
but I already know how the sentence will end.
So I stop her and say
Yo-Soy-Tu-Hija
and I need you to believe in me
or I won't find my way back in.

Tienes razón, Ive,
Mami says, softly,
so soft I almost miss the words,

but then she hugs me

like she used to before the crash,

and maybe things aren't perfect,

but me?

I don't have to be a backup player.

I'm Ive. She's my mami.

Maybe, just maybe,

we can find a way to win.

Mami Stays with Me All Weekend

Like actually takes days off,

eagle eyes on me at all times.

Because we both know Mimi can't be trusted

to watch me

or to help

if things actually got bad.

I kind of hate it, but not too much.

We binge watch the first season

of *One Day at a Time*,

and we talk a little,

plan a little,

for Monday when my suspension is over

and I go back to class.

And so I just write in you, Journal,

catch you up and stuff,

but also for the first time in a while

write some new goals out.

Iveliz Explains It All

- ☐ Talk to Amir
- ☐ Talk to Akiko
- ☐ Talk to Mimi
- ☐ Talk to Mami
- ☐ Talk to My Teachers
- ☐ Talk Talk TALK

A Poem for Amir

Dear Amir,

This should probably be a letter,

but we all know I don't do letters,

I do poems.

Or as Dad would say,

I think I write poems,

but it's all random thoughts and no rhyme.

And I guess what I'm trying to say is,

it's easier to write to you, sometimes,

at least when it's time to confess,

than it is to say things out loud.

I have been a bad friend.

And I convinced myself,

in my head,

that you hated me,

but on the inside I know that that's not right.

You don't hate me. You love me.

And even when I've been at my farthest away,

you've never let go of my hand.

Amir, I am depressed

(yes, I said it),

and this weekend I almost did something bad.

Mami stopped me before I could decide,

and I don't know what would have happened

if she hadn't been around.

I am anxious

and scared

and even though I know talking to you would help me,

all I've done lately is pull back.

The truth is, though,

that I need you.

Because seventh grade is hard enough

without losing my best friend at the same time.

So this is my promise to you:

I will listen more. I will be kind.

I will be there for you when

you need me,

and when I need some time

to cry or be quiet or sad,

I will tell you

actually tell you

and trust you to stay by my side.

I Give Amir the Poem at School

And then I lie down on the grass

while he reads,

my eyes closed,

sunshine on my face,

like I didn't just bare my heart to my friend,

like I don't still think,

deep down,

that he will just tear it up

and go away.

He Doesn't, Of Course

Go away, I mean.
He hugs me
and we talk about the new medicine
Dr. Alex and Dr. Salazar
want me to try,
talk about Mami and me,
and how Dr. Alex wants us to
go to family therapy
to talk about Dad and us and
the things we keep real deep.

I show him the front-door key
that Mimi doesn't have a copy of,
and he tells me about his brother's heart.

Tells me about the hospital,
and the surgery,
and how he wanted me to ask
but didn't want to tell me,
how he grew sadder
as every day
things got worse with him and us.

I even explain about Akiko,
though maybe not all the way.
And he understands perfectly,
maybe all the way.

And by the time the bell rings I feel

lucky, and if not happy,

then for today?

A little bit blessed.

Deep Breaths

When I find Akiko at school,

she looks more hurt than angry,

and even though I immediately get defensive,

I tell my brain to slow down

quiet down

and stop.

I know I undid your makeover,

I say.

AND you yelled Spanish stuff at me in chat,

she throws in.

I knew you were crazy

but what the fudge.

I mean, who even are you?

What'd I even do?

I take a deep breath,

because I don't want to get angry,

I want to explain.

I want to follow my list of goals for once

and see if something can change.

So I say:

Maybe I did do that.

But it felt like you were trying to fix me.

To better me.

Like I wasn't good enough how I was.

And even though I felt kind of uncomfortable,

I didn't know how to tell you to stop.

Akiko frowns. It's called saying no.

You should have said that.

It's only two letters. Only two sounds.

And I wasn't trying to "change" you—

it's a makeover,

and I was just having fun.

I do have trouble saying no,

I admit. But it's hard.

Especially when you're calling me crazy and stuff.

I go to therapy. I have . . .

I have things

I'm working on

and you're just over here

putting me on blast.

I take a deep breath,

because I feel the panic coming up.

My heart beating so loud in my chest

I'm sure kids can hear it

all the way down the hall.

Akiko crosses her arms.

I was just joking. I didn't know you were actually crazy.

Jeez. So sensitive.

Any other words I can't say at all?

And I would normally fake laugh,

especially 'cause I know other kids are around.

But I imagine my dad and stand tall,

breathe deep, and talk Louisiana strong.

It wasn't okay when those kids made fun of your lunch.

Of where you're from.

And it's not okay to make fun of someone for their mental
    health.

For their thoughts.

And if you can't see how they're the same,

then maybe we can't be friends at all.

Mimi's Garden Is Dead

And when I get home,
she is sitting sadly on the balcony,
plucking out the baby seedlings
that just got planted
a little too far into the States.

Lo siento, Mimi,
I tell her,
helping her toss them all
in a Safeway bag.
Because even though I am still angry
and hurt,
I know Mimi's mind is not strong enough,
not right now,
to understand what she did was bad.

Except she reaches out and takes my hand,
her wrinkly one holding me tight,
and she whispers: Tu mamá me lo explicó
y no sé cómo me voy a perdonar.

I stare at our hands, then at her.
Still mostly in shock.
And I don't know if I'm more shocked at
her apology

or the fact that Mami actually listened to me
and they had a talk.
And maybe she mistakes my face for confusion,
because she switches to her accented English
and touches my face.

You are my granddaughter, Ive.
And I would rather you take any medicine in the world
if it'll help you stay here with me
and help me remember
how unbelievably loved I am.

So I nod
and I smile,
and we sit with the dead plants.
And then I suggest maybe we try planting
something a little more American.
Kale, maybe.
¿Algo que en Baltimore se pueda dar?

And Mimi sighs and pats the dirt,
here, but also lost in her mind,
and I wonder if the gandules
were like her letters:
something to remind her
of the soil that she walked on
for sixty-three years of Puerto Rican time.

Mami Corners Me After Dinner

Nervously reminds me
we have family therapy coming up.
Like I could somehow forget
that Dr. Alex is making us talk together,
therapize (?) together,
like that's gonna somehow work and make us bond
and all that.

Still,
I don't run away,
because I am trying,
and when she quiets down
and hands me a dish to dry,
I tell her I am worried about Mimi
and all she left behind.

And that's when Mami gets the idea,
and I mean,
it's not as good as gardening,
but for the first time in a long time,
I see her smile.

Akiko Sits Next to Me at Lunch

And I move around my yuca,
wondering why she came to find me
after everything I said.

But then she takes a deep breath and says:
You were right.
And suddenly I am staring straight at her,
because that is NOT what I expected.

I talked to my mom, she continues.
About what you told me yesterday.
And you're right. I was doing the same things to you
that I was getting mad at other kids
for doing to me.

I was trying to be funny and cool
because, well,
I don't have a lot of friends,
and I didn't realize that my jokes
were actually hurting you instead.

I start to stand up,
'cause I don't think anyone has ever
apologized to me quite like that,
but then Akiko says, BUT—
and I sit my butt back down.

But—

you should have said something sooner,

she says,

shrugging at me

and scuffing her shoe on the floor.

'Cause how am I gonna learn

if nobody talks to me straight?

And I feel annoyance flare up,

'cause it's not my job to teach anybody

anything,

but then Akiko says,

I'm really glad you told me.

Even if it was uncomfortable.

Even if you were scared to come and talk.

And I'd like to still be your friend,

if that's okay with you at all.

Second Chances

I decide to try again with Akiko,

because honestly,

she kind of has a point.

And I wonder how many other people

don't know what they don't know,

until someone is brave enough

to open their mouth.

Mami Picks Me Up After School

And we drive to the rummage store.

It's run by the SPCA people,
and it's like Goodwill,
but all the money goes to cats.

There's an office section in there,
where people dump their old
printers and faxes (?)
and roll-y chairs from OfficeMax.

And it's nice, having an outing together.
It's nice doing something
that's not therapy or fighting,
that's just Mami and me.

And it's there, at four p.m.,
that we find a scanner,
tucked all the way in the back.

I Tell Mimi We Have a New Project

And she looks happy. Surprised.

A mí me encanta pasar tiempo contigo,
mi Tania,
she tells me,
así que tú dime, que yo voy a ayudar.

And my heart hurts for a second,
despite the sweetness of her smile,
because even though she apologized,
I still haven't forgiven how she made me feel
for WEEKS (months?)
when she found out about my pills
and my diagnosis
and the things I do to survive.

Still,
it's one of those days when she thinks I'm Mami,
and even though Mimi's not perfect,
I try to accept every single hug.
Show her how to work the scanner,
and scan the pictures
in a way that tells her
I am someone who loves her
(sin condiciones)
even when her brain is out of luck.

Ghosts

You don't visit me as much anymore,
I tell Dad in my room
when he comes in to kiss me good night.
And he shrugs,
and sits at the edge of my bed,
and strokes my curls in a way
I miss so much
it makes me want to cry.

Am I making you up?
I ask him.
Will you ever go away?
And Dad smiles sadly
and says:
I don't know, honey.
I don't know. 'Cause
I feel like I make you sad,
and you are happier
when I stay away.

You don't make me sad, Dad,
I tell him,
and it's only a little bit of a lie.

Because I am stronger now
than before,
and I am hopeful for my new meds
and my friends
and my old and new lives,
which I am working really hard
to mesh.

School Is Looking Up

By which I mean,
I explained stuff to my teachers
and they're being extra nice.
Because even though this first school quarter
was a roller coaster,
I'm trying out this new talking thing now
and I think if I do just a little better
my semester's grades
may have a shot.

But not just my grades,
my whole experience too.
Because Akiko was right when she said
she wouldn't have been able to change
if she didn't know what not to do,
so even though I'm pretty sure Jessica and Justin G. know
they're awful,
and I'm pretty sure they're not going to change,
Mami still comes with me to talk to the school counselor,
so it's not just me
with a target on the back of my head.

Shutterfly

Mami uploads the scanned pictures,
the ones that gave me the sniffles
from ingesting too much dust
too many times,
and she tells Mimi this
will be the first of many,
because we have plans,
whole bookshelves of photo books
all about her life.

And Mimi?
Her eyes light up.
And she hugs Mami
and me,
and I know it's one of those days
when she can tell, clearly,
which one of us she named,
and which one of us is me.

Laughter

When Amir's brother is finally A-okay better
we celebrate big-time:
pizza, soda, Netflix,
the works.

And Amir,
he opens up his phone
and says he's got something to show me,
a thank-you for listening,
for trying,
even when he knows it's hard.

It's a slam poet I've never heard before—
Elisabet Velasquez—
and she's Puerto Rican like me,
and in the poem she's talking about kids
and their laughter,
how sacred it is.
How free.

And I realize for the first time,
just how long it's been.

How long since I've rolled laughing

from the belly out

and hiccupped from giggling

not crying,

smiling

from within.

But maybe

it's coming.

Maybe

it's already here.

Maybe

I just need to keep talking

keep loving

keep letting people in.

My Journal Is Almost Full

And I think I am going to take a break
before I ask Mami for another.

I have so much therapy coming up,
alone and with Mami,
that it may be time to practice speaking
just a little bit more
and writing
just a little bit less.

I mean,
writing is good,
but I'm discovering I also like my voice.
I kind of like explaining myself
with my whole body,
and not hiding in paper,
where I can turn the page
the minute I need that choice.

¿Y quién sabe?
Knowing me,
it might make me an even better poet,
more riveting for my future fans.
¿Estás ready, mi audiencia?
'Cause Journal 2?
It's coming with a bang.

Epilogue

How long has it been, Journal?
Months?
It's hard to believe I've been absent so long.

And I'm not gonna lie to you,
because I said I'd stop doing that—
it's not all perfect,
and I'm not suddenly the happiest girl on the block.

But you know what?
Today I asked Mami if we could make an album,
like the ones we did for Mimi,
but just of her and me and Dad.

And Mami said:
¿Por qué no escribes unos poemitas
de nuestras memorias
y los metemos ahí entre las fotos
para variar?

And yes, Mami and I still struggle to talk,
and therapy with her is not easy.
But I am learning to accept her love
and she is learning to trust mine,
and her asking me to write poems for the album?

It just goes to show that all this feeling work

is slowly paying off over time.

And when Dad visits me?

De vez en cuando,

just casually stopping by?

I show him Mimi's and my kale

and our photo albums,

and I tell him about therapy

and the new pills

that are finally getting it right.

Sometimes Mimi even sees me smiling,

and she nods wisely and crosses her chest.

¿Tu ángel guardián? she asks.

And I smile at her and Mami

and think how lucky I am

to finally be seen

by people who understand.

Author's Note

Dear Reader,

Although this book is a work of fiction, it shows what many kids and teens go through every day.

I hope you can take something positive away from Iveliz's story. If a friend or family member needs your help, I hope you feel like you can better support them. And if you saw yourself in Iveliz, I hope she inspires you to be brave and ask for help when you need it. I hope this book shows you that you are not alone and that there is nothing wrong with you. And that sometimes, when we ask for help, things can and do get better.

I also know, though, that we don't all have access to the same things. That maybe you might not be able to go to therapy, or maybe you aren't ready to talk to someone in your real life. I get it. Therapy usually costs money, and it depends on you getting permission from adults. And trusting people? I know how scary that can feel—it's not an easy thing to do.

I've listed some resources that might help you (or one of your friends) get through a hard time. I hope they can help you take the next step in understanding your own mental health or that of someone you know.

Thank you for reading, friend. Really. Iveliz and I are glad you're here.

Love,
Andrea

Resources

I know sometimes it's hard to tell people in your real life what's going on. But it's also important to reach out when you need help, like Iveliz did in this book. If you know you need to talk to someone but you're not ready to talk to an adult you know, you can call the Boys Town National Hotline at **1-800-448-3000** or text **VOICE** to **20121** any day at any time. It's a number meant just for kids and teens like you.

There are also many good videos on YouTube you can use to learn more about yourself or simply to listen to other kids and teens who are going through similar things. These are some of my favorites:

We All Have Mental Health (Anna Freud NCCF)
youtube.com/watch?v=DxIDKZHW3-E

You Are Not Your Thoughts (AboutKidsHealth)
youtube.com/watch?v=0QXmmP4psbA

Healthy Head to Toe: Kids Explain Anxiety and Depression (The Oregonian)
youtube.com/watch?v=dZgMvyRkaI4

If you're not a video-watching kind of person but prefer to read quietly, check out the KidsHealth website. This page has a lot of good info on emotions and how to handle them in different situations: kidshealth.org/en/kids/feeling.

And if all of this has made you feel empowered and you want to help create a safe space for kids or teens at your school to talk about mental health, why not start a club? Erika's Lighthouse is a website with a lot of good ideas and resources for getting started: erikaslighthouse.org/teen-empowerment.

Acknowledgments

I have been writing for as long as I can remember, and if there is one positive thing that came out of this pandemic (for me), it's that I found people who believed in my work and helped me make my dreams come true.

The biggest and most loving thank-you goes to my agent, Rebecca Eskildsen. I can still remember how floored I was, how grateful, when I saw the amount of care and time you put into your initial feedback email, not even knowing if you'd ever hear from me again. I knew right then that you'd be Iveliz's best and most nurturing advocate, and I can't thank you enough for all you did to help me land my deal and for all you've done for me since.

To my amazing editor, Tricia Lin, who brought me into the folds of Random House and never stopped gushing about how much she loved my book. Thank you for your careful edits, and for helping Iveliz really shine. My book has grown exponentially since passing through your hands.

And of course to everyone else who helped my book become what it is. To Katrina Damkoehler and Ken Crossland, for their wonderful visions of what my cover and interior pages should look like, and to Abigail Dela Cruz for the cover art of my dreams. Thank you also to Alyssa Bermudez, for the perfect interior art, and to Barbara Bakowski and Nancee Adams for catching all the little typos and repeated words that none of the rest of us saw. Finally, a thank-you to Rebecca Vitkus, Caroline Abbey, Michelle Nagler, Mallory Loehr, Kris Kam, Dominique Cimina, and John Adamo and the rest of the marketing team for helping get Iveliz's story out there to be loved and seen.

Writing doesn't happen in isolation, though, and so I also need to thank my amazing IRL partner and friends, who've supported me from day one. To Kris, who, in addition to coming up with the title for this story, read multiple drafts and (virtually) held my hand through the entire querying, submission, and publishing process. To Chaka, my loving boosky and fellow dog parent, who proposed soon after I got my book deal and really made sure summer 2021 was one to remember. And, of course, to my OLL/Brindlewood/Octopus crew, Tashay and Amanda, who kept me going via grandma detective role-playing, romance books, and the sweetest, most loving texts.

Moreover, huge thanks to my Bookstagram community, whom I friended while posting about other people's books but who have also cheered me on throughout my writing journey. Special thanks to Amparo Ortiz, my amazing (unofficial) author mentor; Iris, my official hype friend; the OGs (like Wilmarie and Mari), who supported my very first self-published stuff; the #WeLoveMG Book Club crew (so glad you asked me to run it with you, Ale); the Sunshine Teacher Buddies group, for getting me through another teaching year; and finally, the now-defunct Freakytonas, ha-ha.

In a book about mental health, I also need to thank the therapists I've met over the years. To Angela, for counseling me through some of the hardest times in my life and always lifting me up. To Alex, Bre, Michelle, and Teri, for being there for the young ladies I've loved with all my heart. And, of course, to Dr. Dwonna D. Thompson-Lenoir, for reading my book and making sure all the therapy scenes were accurate and made sense.

Finally, to my family. To my siblings and aunts and uncles, for always encouraging me, even if what I was talking about sounded weird as heck. To my grandparents, Babi y Nonno, who are no longer here but would make me the biggest celebratory dinner if they were. And to my other grandparents, Abi y Abo, who *are* here and still give me the warmest hugs.

Last but not least, to my mami, a quien amo con todo mi corazón. Gracias por siempre apoyarme y creer que alcanzaría mis sueños no importa que. Gracias por hacerme reír cuando hablamos por las mañanas, y por ponerme presión para escribir. Sabes que el próximo libro viene para ti. ♥